ADVENTURE G

Suspects!

Stephen Thraves

Illustrated by Peter Dennis

HODDER AND STOUGHTON
LONDON SYDNEY AUCKLAND TORONTO

British Library Cataloguing in Publication Data

Thraves, Stephen
Suspects! – (who-done-it adventure game book)
1. Fantasy role-playing games
I. Title II. Series
793.93

ISBN 0-340-54871-1

First published 1991

Published by Hodder and Stoughton Children's Books, a division of Hodder and Stoughton Ltd,
Mill Road, Dunton Green, Sevenoaks, Kent TN13 2YA

Photoset by Rowland Phototypesetting Ltd,
Bury St Edmunds, Suffolk

Printed in Great Britain by BPCC Hazel Books,
Aylesbury, Bucks, England
Member of BPCC Ltd

How good a detective are you? Good enough to spot all the clues and work out who on the elegant Olympic Express is the murderer? Well, let's hope you are. If you don't identify the murderer quickly enough, he or she may well make YOU their next victim!

There wasn't meant to be a murder on the famous Athens to Paris express. At least, not a *real* murder. A film team had chartered the beautiful old-fashioned train to shoot some sequences for a who-done-it film. But as the Olympic Express crossed a deep ravine in the Alps the film's director was pushed out of a carriage door. Who sent him to his doom? YOU are the detective who is appointed to board the train to try and find out.

It's not going to be an easy task. The director was a very difficult and unpleasant man and every *one* of the film team had good reason for wanting to dispose of him. He had continually upset them all: he had called Tom Henson and Jacqui Dean (the male and female stars) talentless, Giles Blade and Iris Carter (the male and female character actors) lazy, and Bob Adams and Nick Todd (the cameraman and sound man) incompetent. He'd said that he would make sure that none of them ever found work again!

So any one of the six suspects could be the murderer. In fact it will be someone different every time you play the game, for the game is devised so that no two investigations you undertake are ever the same . . . each involving different murderers, incidents and clues.

The game can therefore be played again and again – as many times as you like!

HOW TO PLAY

The playing pieces contained in this wallet are as follows: three double-sided DETECTIVE'S NOTEBOOK cards; a PHOTOGRAPH OF SUSPECTS card; a SPECIAL DICE; 4 coloured CLUE cards (red, yellow, blue, green); 1 black SOLUTION card; and a COUNTER (to record attempts on your life by the murderer).

First of all, select one of the DETECTIVE'S NOTEBOOK cards and select one side of this card. Keep this card near you, with that side uppermost. The other two DETECTIVE'S NOTEBOOK cards will not be required in this game and so can be returned to the wallet.

The DETECTIVE'S NOTEBOOK card you have chosen hides the name of the murderer for this game. It is one of the six suspects shown on the PHOTOGRAPH OF SUSPECTS card. So keep this card near you as well for ready reference. You can study this 'photograph' as often as you like during the game.

Every so often during the book you will come across a picture in the middle of a paragraph, illustrating that part of the story. Study that picture very carefully because at the next page you turn to you will be asked a question about it. The difficulty of that question is decided by throwing the SPECIAL DICE: the gun symbol means a hard question, the dagger symbol a medium question, and the poison bottle an easy question.

If you get the answer to the question correct (shown by an upturned thumb 👍 at the answer paragraph you choose), you will on some – but not all! – occasions receive a clue about the murderer. If you *are* to receive a clue, the book will tell you that you are entitled to select one of the coloured CLUE cards. You place the coloured CLUE card that you have chosen over your DETECTIVE'S NOTEBOOK card, making sure that the notebook shapes on each are exactly aligned. Your clue will then appear in your DETECTIVE'S NOTEBOOK! So if, for example, the word 'pullover' appears there, it means that the murderer is one of the suspects wearing a pullover.

You can pick up further CLUE cards by correctly answering

other picture questions in the book. Each coloured CLUE card will enable you to eliminate one or more of the suspects. For example, if your first CLUE card tells you that the murderer wears trainers you can eliminate Iris Carter, since she has high heels. If your second CLUE card tells you that the murderer is dark then Bob Adams and Nick Todd can be eliminated as well . . . and so on.

Once you have picked up a particular CLUE card you can remind yourself of this clue (i.e. by placing the CLUE card over the DETECTIVE'S NOTEBOOK card) as often as you like. But, obviously, you are not allowed to use those coloured CLUE cards that you haven't yet picked up.

You win the game by correctly naming the murderer. Naming the murderer can be done at any point in the game but you are only allowed one attempt at this. You check if you are right by placing the black SOLUTION card over your DETECTIVE'S NOTEBOOK card. If it's not the suspect you thought, then you have failed.

The only way to be *sure* of naming the murderer correctly is to collect all **four** CLUE cards. This will enable you to eliminate all of the suspects except one. So you should aim to collect as many CLUE cards as possible. This must be done before the train reaches Paris, its destination. The game ends here and you will therefore be asked to make a guess at the murderer whether you have all of the clues or not.

There's something else that you must watch out for when collecting clues. The murderer will try to thwart your investigation, making various attempts at bumping YOU off! You risk such an attempt on those occasions when you answer a picture question wrongly (shown by a downturned thumb at the answer paragraph you choose); although not *every* wrong answer will necessarily result in a murder attempt.

All murder attempts should be recorded on the movable COUNTER. You start the game with ***zero*** showing through the window of the COUNTER, so rotate the disc until **0** appears. For each murder attempt, you turn the dial clockwise until the next number shows. You manage to survive the first two attempts but the third, unfortunately, proves fatal. So when **3** shows through the window of the COUNTER, the game is over for you even *before* the express has reached its destination.

However, you are still allowed a 'dying breath' chance to name the murderer. You will be asked to make your guess immediately, using what clues you have.

Whether you have won the game or not, you may well want to play it again. To do this, shuffle the three DETECTIVE'S NOTEBOOK cards and select one for your next murder investigation. It will probably be a different murderer this time . . . but, even if it isn't, you won't know until you've collected the four CLUE cards again!

READY TO START . . .

YOU had originally gone to Innsbruck in Austria to do some skiing but you now find yourself being hurriedly driven to the railway station. 'I am sorry for interrupting your holiday here,' the local police inspector apologises, as he's careful not to let his car skid on the icy roads, 'but we've heard what a brilliant private detective you are. We were wondering if you would help out with this baffling murder case. It happened a couple of hours ago – on the famous Olympic Express! We would be grateful if you would join the train for the rest of its journey to Paris to try and find out who committed the foul deed!'

By the time you reach Innsbruck railway station, the inspector has briefly given you all the details of the murder. The victim was Larry Frost, the famous film director, and he was pushed from the train some fifty miles south of Innsbruck as it crossed a deep ravine in the Italian Alps. Apart from the train's staff, the only people on board were the rest of the film team: Tom Henson, Jacqui Dean, Giles Blade, Iris Carter, Bob Adams and Nick Todd. The inspector hands you a group photograph of these six people, telling you that the murderer must be one of them!

So are you tempted by this intriguing case? If you are, you had better hurry through to the platform because the Olympic Express is just about to depart for the next stage of its long journey. There's just time for me to wish you luck before you turn the page . . .

1

'Welcome to the Olympic Express!' a man in a black jacket says, greeting you as you quickly climb aboard one of the elegant maroon carriages. He wears a bow tie beneath a wing collar and there is gold braid on his shoulders. 'My name is Pierre, I'm the chief steward. You must be the clever detective they were trying to get hold of. Oh, this is a terrible business! To think that there was a murder on this train just an hour ago – and that the murderer is still on board somewhere! I will of course do everything I can to help in your investigation. But, first, let me show you to your cabin.' You tell Pierre that the cabin can wait for later, though – you want to start your enquiry as soon as possible. 'Anything you say,' he replies obligingly as the train now starts to jerk out of Innsbruck station. 'Where can I take you first? Mr Frost's cabin . . . the door through which he was pushed . . . or where he was last seen?'

If you prefer Frost's cabin	go to 35
If you prefer the fatal door	go to 302
If you prefer where Frost last seen	go to 176

2

On which side of Giles's cup was his spoon?

If you think on window side	go to 131
If you think on aisle side	go to 262

3

Your thoughts are interrupted by a faint knock on the cabin door. 'Come in!' you call out, assuming this to be Pierre returning to make sure that everything is to your satisfaction. The door remains closed, however, and so you call out again, rather louder this time. But still no one enters. Wondering if Pierre is slightly deaf, you stand up to open the door yourself. 'That's strange,' you remark to yourself as you wander out into the corridor, peering to left and right, 'there's not a soul in sight!' As you turn your head to the left again, however, a bullet hisses past your cheek from behind you. That knock had obviously come from the murderer . . . to lure you into a trap!

Record this murder attempt on your COUNTER. Now go to 81.

4

Which object on Iris and Giles's table was nearest the champagne bucket?

If you think plate of crisps	go to 117
If you think drinks menu	go to 67
If you think ashtray	go to 168

5

As you observe Bob and Nick strolling to the right end of the platform, you notice how edgy Nick looks. He keeps looking nervously over his shoulder. You wonder if this means that he's about to make a run for it and he's checking that no one is watching him! But perhaps there's a very different reason for Nick's edginess. Perhaps he has worked out that *Bob* was the one who pushed Larry Frost off the train and he's worried that Bob might have guessed this. Perhaps his nervousness is because he's afraid

that Bob might try to bump *him* off next! You watch at your window even more carefully now because the express lets out a shrill whistle to show that it's about to start moving again. Nick reboards it immediately . . . but why is Bob Adams suddenly walking the other direction, towards the back of the platform? Is he about to make his getaway? But, no, he is merely walking over to the chocolate machine. As soon as he has obtained his chocolate bar, he hurries back to the train, jumping on just as it starts to pull out. With a relieved sigh, you lie back in your cosy seat and try to remember what you have just seen at the station . . .

Throw the SPECIAL DICE to test your memory, then turn

to the appropriate number.

If thrown go to 239

If thrown go to 64

If thrown go to 169

6

How many of the sweets on Bob's seat were between the sweet packet and the pair of spectacles?

If you think none go to 103
If you think one go to 238
If you think two go to 272
If you think three go to 27

7

When you have finished questioning those three suspects resting in their cabins, you return to your own cabin to consider their answers. Was Giles Blade the murderer? Or was it Iris Carter or Bob Adams? Or was it *none* of these three – but one of those other suspects elsewhere on the train? You're starting to consider a few theories but you haven't formulated anything concrete yet. You hope your next round of interviews – with Tom, Jacqui and Nick – might give you the missing pieces you need. That is, of course, as long as the murderer doesn't manage to deal with you first! ***Go to 282.***

8

How far down did the cord on the window blind hang?

To above oval wall plaques	go to 260
To middle of oval wall plaques	go to 244
To bottom of oval wall plaques	go to 99

9

'Who is it?' a nervous voice asks from inside as you knock on Iris Carter's door. 'You can't come in until you announce yourself!' So you do as she asks, telling her that you're the detective. 'I thought you might be the murderer,' she explains as you find her huddled in the corner of her cabin. 'I really won't be happy until he's been caught. I'm frightened that he might strike one of us next! Say he thinks that one of us *saw* him push Lawrence off the train . . . and he wants to make sure that we don't talk!' It seems a very convincing display of nerves by Miss Carter but you're not totally

taken in by it. After all, she did *know* that you would soon be coming to question her. Perhaps she had that little act all prepared! 'You speak of the murderer as a *he*, Miss Carter,' you point out to her.

'How do you know that it wasn't a *she*? Did you witness anything by any chance?' She quickly shakes her head, though. 'No, the reason I didn't say *she*,' she explains, 'is that, apart from myself, the only she on this train is Jacqui. I'm sure it couldn't have been her!' Thinking this statement over, you soon excuse yourself from Miss Carter's cabin. You hope you have correctly remembered everything about it.

Throw the SPECIAL DICE – then turn to the appropriate number.

If	 (gun)	thrown	go to 104
If	 (dagger)	thrown	go to 237
If	 (poison)	thrown	go to 26

10

On which segment of Tom's suitcase was the ATHENS sticker?

If you think left segment	go to 73
If you think middle segment	go to 141
If you think right segment	go to 184

11

It's almost an hour later when you finally complete your interviews with the three remaining suspects. But it now means that you have at last spoken to everyone. Does it also mean that you are definitely able to say who the murderer is, then? No, unfortunately, it does not. You've still got a lot more thinking to do! As you are making your way back to your cabin, you pass the door where that terrible incident took place. Taking a closer look at it, you suddenly notice that there are some scratch marks near the handle. Then you realise that they are more than marks – they're rough letters and they make up a word! Larry Frost must have desperately scratched the word with his ring or something during the struggle. For it is clearly a *clue* about the murderer!

You may pick up one of the coloured CLUE cards. Place this exactly over your DETECTIVE'S NOTEBOOK card to find out what the scratched word is. Now go to 47.

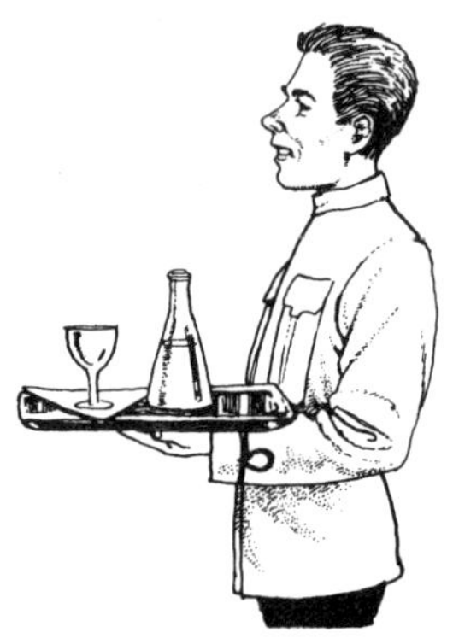

12

The bottom magazine on the table in the observation car was entitled YACHTING. But you could only see part of this title. How much?

If you think the letters *TING*	go to 284
If you think the letters *HTING*	go to 123
If you think the letters *CHTING*	go to 174
If you think the letters *ACHTING*	go to 212

13

Returning to your cabin after interviewing those three suspects in the dining-car, you notice that, strangely, an envelope has appeared on your seat! Curious, you slit it open to read what's inside. There's a note in there, folded round a photograph. You examine the note first. It reads: 'I'm one of your suspects but I daren't reveal myself in case the murderer finds out. I was taking a few snaps of the passing scenery with my Polaroid camera when I spotted the back of the murderer at the other end of the corridor.

He or she had just pushed Larry Frost out of the door! I immediately hid in the nearest washroom, so I didn't have time to study the person. But I must have accidentally pressed the button on my camera because, ten seconds later, this photo developed itself!' You now eagerly turn your attention to the photograph. Although it's very blurred, there's no doubt that it's genuine. You can just about see Larry Frost disappearing out of the door . . . and there's a vague clue about the murderer!

You may pick up one of the coloured CLUE cards. Place this exactly over your DETECTIVE'S NOTEBOOK card to find out what this photographic clue is. Now go to 47.

14

Where precisely were the ice-bucket tongs at the back of the bar?

Under mirror	go to 260
To one side of mirror	go to 200

15

Feeling very tense, you slip through the end door of the dining-car yourself and creep towards the kitchen-car. Passing the washroom on your left, you anxiously wonder whether the murderer is hiding in there instead. But then you notice that the word 'vacant' is showing above the handle. This means that the door hasn't been locked. Surely it *would* be locked if the murderer was hiding in there. So you slowly continue towards the kitchen-car, fairly confident now that your escape hasn't been cut off. Finally reaching the door of the kitchen-car, you very gradually pull it open a fraction. Through this opening you see a set of knives hanging on

the far wall, and you are relieved to note that none is missing. If the murderer was hiding behind the door, he would surely have armed himself with one of the knives! If you are right about that, though, you certainly weren't right about the washroom, for you suddenly hear its door open behind you and someone rush out and dart back through the dining-car. The murderer was in there after all . . . and you've let him or her escape. As you dart back through the train yourself, you wonder if you have remembered all the details about the kitchen correctly.

Throw the SPECIAL DICE to check.

If	(gun)	thrown	go to 48
If	(dagger)	thrown	go to 153
If	(poison)	thrown	go to 295

16

Which item on the table was nearest to the wine glass?

If you think sauce-boat	go to 260
If you think cork	go to 99
If you think wine bottle	go to 244

17

Waiting until the express is well out of Zurich station, you make a visit to the washroom along your corridor. After washing your hands, you reach down to the little drawer at one side of the basin for a clean towel. As you open the towel, something suddenly drops out on to the floor. Picking it up, you see that it's Larry Frost's diary! He must have hidden it in the stack of towels some time before he was pushed off the train. But *why*, you wonder. You receive the answer when you open the diary . . . ***Go to 214.***

18

How many objects were on the table in the cabin?

If you think one	go to 260
If you think two	go to 99
If you think three	go to 200
If you think four	go to 244

19

As you now examine the fatal door, the one through which the film director was pushed, you ask Pierre if he saw anyone in this corridor after he went to investigate the scream. His face becomes quite grave. 'Yes, I did,' he says, nodding slowly. 'Only a fleeting glance, unfortunately, because he or she was just disappearing into the next carriage along. This person must have been the murderer, though. I have no doubts about that!' Tense, you eagerly ask Pierre if he is able to give you any clue about what the murderer looked like. Again, he slowly nods his head . . .

You may pick up one of the coloured CLUE cards. Place this exactly over your DETECTIVE'S NOTEBOOK card to find out Pierre's clue. Now go to 61.

20

Where was the handle on the fatal door?

Between top and second safety bar	go to 130
Between second and third safety bar	go to 63

21

You decide it's now time to meet the other passengers on the train – the suspects! – and you ask Pierre where you might find them. 'They're all in the dining-car at the moment,' he replies. 'They're taking afternoon tea. Please follow me.' As Pierre steps back to allow you to enter the dining-car first, your immediate observation is how elegant the carriage is. There's a little table at each window, with a pink-shaded lamp and a tiny vase of flowers. It's only afterwards that you properly take note of the people sitting there. At the nearest table is Jacqui Dean and Tom Henson; at the next, Iris Carter and Bob Adams; at the furthest, Giles Blade and Nick Todd. Which table should you approach first?

If you prefer Jacqui and Tom's	go to 226
If you prefer Iris and Bob's	go to 190
If you prefer Giles and Nick's	go to 115

22

Which object was immediately in front of Tom's plate?

If you think teacup	go to 137
If you think mustard boat	go to 53
If you think salt- and pepper-pots	go to 192

23

At the very end of that carriage Pierre unlocks a door. 'Will this be suitable for you?' he asks as he ushers you into an exquisitely-decorated cabin. He knows that he doesn't have to wait for an answer, though, and respectfully withdraws so you can make yourself comfortable in there. You've barely had time to test how cosy the seats are, however, when you hear a faint knock. Assuming that this is Pierre again, you stand up to open the door. Suddenly, three holes appear in the wood, accompanied by three loud cracks. Someone in the corridor must have fired a gun at it! You are very fortunate that you hadn't quite moved to the centre of the door or you would have been hit!

Record this murder attempt on your COUNTER. Now go to 81.

24

Above which of the family sitting on the platform bench was the ski poster?

If you think the boy	go to 79
If you think the girl	go to 208
If you think the father	go to 180
If you think the mother	go to 252

25

Finding Giles Blade's cabin, you politely knock on the door. A pity his reply isn't as polite! 'What is it, what is it?' he shouts rudely. 'Not more pestering with fruit or clean towels, is it? Oh, do come in, man!' He obviously assumed you to be a steward but when he sees that you are not his manner doesn't change at all. 'Oh, it's *you*!' he snarls, no less rude. 'Haven't you worked out who the murderer is yet? I wish you would hurry up about it so we can all be left in peace. Come on, then. What stupid questions do you want to ask?' You refuse to be provoked by Giles Blade's rudeness, though, politely asking him who *he* thinks disposed of the director. 'You're asking

me?' he exclaims sarcastically. 'Well, a fine detective you are, asking the suspects! But if you must have my view, I think it was probably Nick Todd. That young man might look very mild on the surface but he's got a lot of pride. He doesn't like being pushed around. And I don't like being bothered! So is that all?' You tell him that it *is* all for the moment and leave his unpleasant company. As you search along the corridors for the cabins of those other suspects, you try to commit the detail of Giles's cabin to memory.

Throw the SPECIAL DICE to test your memory.

If [gun] thrown go to 263

If [dagger] thrown go to 120

If [poison bottle] thrown go to 56

26

What object on the table was nearest the umbrella in Iris's cabin?

If you think glass	go to 91
If you think decanter	go to 57

27

In all, you managed to find three suspects in their cabins. The other three – Nick, Tom and Jacqui – must be in either one of the communal carriages or hiding from you somewhere! As you are returning to your own cabin, you notice that one of the corridor washrooms is engaged. You knock gently on the door to see who replies. Since there's no answer, you tactfully leave it a couple of minutes and then knock again. Still there's no answer – but then the door starts gradually to open. As it creaks open wider and wider, you eagerly wonder which of the suspects is about to step out. He or she is certainly acting very furtively for some reason! But it's not Nick, Tom or Jacqui who eventually appears. It's Pierre. He was just checking that no new towels or soap were required in the washroom! ***Go to 282.***

28

How many of the curtains visible on the train were tied back?

If you think one	go to 172
If you think two	go to 234
If you think three	go to 280

29

'I'm sorry to intrude upon your dinner, Miss Dean,' you apologise as you walk up to her, 'but I wondered if I might join you at your table. I'd like to ask you a question or two.' As you take the empty seat opposite Jacqui, you notice her put down her soupspoon – even though the soup-bowl is more than half full still. You feel rather embarrassed by this. 'Oh, please feel free to continue eating while we talk,' you tell her. But Jacqui insists that she was about to leave the rest of her soup anyway. 'I don't want to ruin my beautiful

figure!' she says vainly. 'Now what is it you wanted to ask? How much did I dislike Larry Frost, I suppose. The answer is a lot!' This *was* in fact the main question you wanted to ask her – and you now enquire *why* she disliked him so much. 'Because he was always telling me that I had no talent,' she replies huffily. 'He said that I was merely a beautiful face. The cheek of the man! About my lack of talent, I mean. He was right about my face, of course!' Jacqui's main course now arrives at her table and you decide to let her enjoy it in peace. As you move on to one of the other tables, you test your memory on what you have just observed . . .

Throw the SPECIAL DICE – then turn to appropriate number.

If	[gun]	thrown	go to 84
If	[dagger]	thrown	go to 126
If	[poison bottle]	thrown	go to 247

30

How many lamps were visible in the corridor when Nick was talking to you?

If you think three	go to 258
If you think four	go to 144
If you think five	go to 11
If you think six	go to 97

31

Half an hour or so after the train has left Zurich, a steward knocks on your cabin door. 'I've just come to wish you goodnight,' he tells you in a loud voice. Then his voice drops to a whisper so he can tell you the *real* reason he has paid you a visit. He nervously checks over his shoulder. 'Not long before Mr Frost was pushed off the train,' he confides into your ear, 'I heard him shouting at someone in his cabin. He was telling that person not to threaten him. As I passed his cabin, the door was open and I got a slight glimpse of the person. I thought I'd tell you what I know because I am sure he or she was the murderer!'

You may pick up one of the coloured CLUE cards. Place this

exactly over the DETECTIVE'S NOTEBOOK card to find out what the steward has to tell you about the murderer. Now go to 224.

32

Was the umbrella lying above or below the level of the lock on the cage door?

If you think above	go to 260
If you think below	go to 200

33

As it gets later and later into the night, you decide you won't be totally safe until you have left the train. You are sure the murderer will do his or her utmost to bump you off over the next few hours! For the umpteenth time you jump up to make sure that your cabin door is properly bolted. But then you realise that the best way to protect yourself against the murderer is to name him or her as quickly as possible. Then you can get everyone else on the train to help keep guard over that person. So you really need to collect some more clues! The obvious course of action is to revisit that carriage door where the murder actually took place. But that would mean leaving the safety of your cabin . . . ***Go to 127.***

34

Where was the case with the wheels at the bottom?

If you think on top shelf	go to 244
If you think on bottom shelf	go to 260
If you think on floor	go to 99

35

'Mr Frost's cabin is right at the end,' Pierre informs you as you follow him into thc ncxt carriage and then along the narrow corridor. 'Here we are,' he says eventually, taking out his passkey when you have both arrived at the last of the beautiful mahogany doors. Unlocking the door, he ushers you into the cabin. You take a quick look round the small but sumptuous compartment, noticing the film clapperboard on the seat. 'Has anything in here been touched since Mr Frost was pushed off the train?' you ask Pierre

thoughtfully. The chief steward shakes his head. 'Oh no – I can give you my word on that,' he replies. 'I locked this door as soon as I heard about Mr Frost's murder. And I'm the only one with the passkey.' When you have finished investigating the cabin, you ask

Pierre to lock the door again. 'Perhaps you could now show me to my own cabin,' you ask him. Pierre obligingly leads you to the other end of the corridor, opening the door on another lavish compartment. After he has gone, you make yourself comfortable by the window, staring out at the beautiful mountain scenery. As you stare out, you try to recall a detail about Larry Frost's cabin . . .

Throw the SPECIAL DICE to decide what sort of detail.

If		thrown	go to 167
If		thrown	go to 261
If		thrown	go to 229

36

What on the table was furthest away from the chair in which Larry Frost sat?

If you think menu	go to 268
If you think butter-dish	go to 87
If you think bread-basket	go to 154
If you think napkin	go to 19

37

As you continue along the corridor towards your cabin, you realise that your answer was *wrong* about that detail. You now remember the correct answer! Tutting at yourself, you enter your cabin and sit down next to the window. You hope the passing scenery might give you some inspiration. You're so busy staring out at it that you fail to notice the slight opening of the cabin door. But you *do* notice the barrel of a gun suddenly appearing there . . . just in time! You quickly duck as a couple of shots are fired from it. If you had been a fraction slower, they would have hit you!

Record this murder attempt on your COUNTER. Now go to 81.

38

Was Tom drinking white or red wine?

If you think white go to 117
If you think red go to 67

39

The express has soon reached full speed again, its sparks reflecting in the snow. As you stare out at this attractive sight, your thoughts again return to the murderer. Surely that person would have to be quite strong to have pushed Larry Frost out of the door? So that should rule out the two women, Iris and Jacqui . . . *and* the feeble-looking Nick Todd, for that matter! But perhaps the murderer possessed a gun as well and used *this* to coax Larry towards the opened door. If that was the case, then it didn't matter whether the murderer was particularly strong or not! ***Go to 222.***

40

Which object on table was nearest to Giles?

If you think water decanter	go to 27
If you think travel-clock	go to 272
If you think glass	go to 238

41

By the time you have completed your interviews with those suspects resting in their cabins and have returned to your own cabin, it has gone completely dark outside. You therefore walk over to the small lamp under the window to provide yourself with a little more light. The murderer must have slipped into your cabin during your absence, however, and tampered with the lamp. As you try to switch it on, you receive an electric shock! Will you recover from it?

Record this murder attempt on your COUNTER. Now go to 282. (Remember: when there have been three murder attempts against you, this game is over and you must guess the murderer immediately.)

42

Which object on the pull-out table was nearest to Giles?

Miniature brandy bottle	go to 91
Travel-clock	go to 160
Book	go to 254
Glass	go to 57

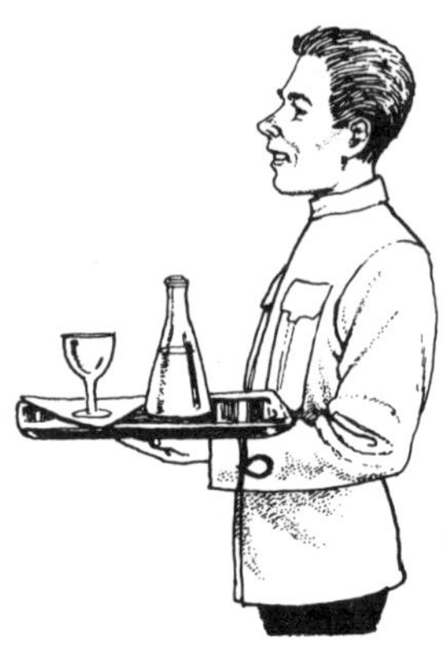

43

It takes longer to warm up than you expect and so you ring the little bell in your cabin to order some hot coffee. 'I'm sorry I've been so long,' the steward apologises when he knocks on your door some quarter of an hour later, 'but every member of the film team suddenly wanted coffee as well! Altogether, I've had to deliver *seven* coffee pots from this tray. Thankfully, you're the last!' That fact should have made you worry about your coffee – you should have realised that one of the film team could have quickly added something to your pot when taking their own from the tray. But you sip your coffee without thinking. It's only *afterwards* that you realise it could be poison. You realise because suddenly you can taste it!

Record this murder attempt on your COUNTER. Now go to 142.

44

Was the barman in the cocktail-car holding the cloth in his left or right hand?

If you think in his left	go to 97
If you think in his right	go to 11

45

Walking along to the cocktail-car, you find that Nick Todd and the barman are the only two in there at the moment. But they are not talking to each other. Nick is sitting silently and miserably staring into his glass of lager. 'Oh, hello!' Nick mumbles at you as you take a seat next to him. 'I know I really shouldn't be drinking until you have questioned me but I promise you I am still perfectly sober. I feel so shaken by this terrible business that I don't think I could get drunk even if I tried!' After ordering a drink for yourself – a lemonade with a dash of lime juice – you confide to Nick that you

are still some way from being able to name the murderer. You ask him if *he* has any theories as to who it might be. 'All I can tell you is that it's not me,' he replies quietly. 'I suppose I would like to think that it's Giles Blade – because he's so very unpleasant. But I don't really have any evidence for thinking it's him.' As you leave the cocktail-car a few minutes later, you are very tempted to eliminate Nick from your list of suspects. He sounds so sincere – but perhaps he's just very crafty! So you try to remember as much as you can about what you have observed . . .

Throw the SPECIAL DICE – then turn to the appropriate number.

If thrown go to 257

If thrown go to 58

If thrown go to 163

46

How many words on the menu at Tom's table began with the letter S?

If you think one go to 164
If you think two go to 13
If you think three go to 71

47

An hour passes in your cabin . . . then two . . . but you still seem to be getting nowhere in trying to work out the identity of the murderer. The problem is that *every one of the suspects* despised Larry Frost – and so *every one of the suspects* had a motive! And they all seem to have had the opportunity, too, for not one of the six suspects is able to produce a proper alibi for the time Larry Frost was pushed off the train. Anxiously glancing at your watch, you see that it is nearly midnight now. That means you have less than nine hours to work out this problem as you will have reached Paris by that time and, unless you have some concrete proof, you will not be able to prevent all the suspects from leaving the train! ***Go to 188.***

48

Which of the knives hanging from the kitchen-car wall was the shortest?

Knife nearest to pans	go to 200
Knife second nearest to pans	go to 244
Knife second furthest away from pans	go to 99
Knife furthest away from pans	go to 260

49

You are about to open the door to cabin 1 when you realise that the murderer might be standing in there pointing a gun at you! So you prudently step to one side of the door, reaching across for the handle. You slowly turn it, then nudge the door open with your foot. You hold your breath, waiting for a sudden shot. There isn't one, though, and so it seems safe to step into the doorway. You do so cautiously, however, prepared to leap back again if necessary. To your relief, you see that the cabin is empty. Noticing all the boxes on the floor and the piles of blankets on the seats, you assume that it is temporarily being used as a storeroom. Stepping a little further into the cabin you see that the boxes contain spare vases and water

decanters. It's then that the door is suddenly shut behind you. You open it just in time to see the murderer's dark shape disappear down the end of the corridor. He or she has given you the slip! As you race down the corridor yourself, you test your memory on what you have just seen in the cabin. You hope the mental exercise might ease your nerves a little!

Throw the SPECIAL DICE – then turn to the appropriate number.

If		thrown	go to 60
If		thrown	go to 8
If		thrown	go to 112

50

In which direction was the umbrella handle pointing?

If you think towards tennis rackets	go to 260
If you think away from tennis rackets	go to 200

51

Feeling very curious, you make your way back to Larry Frost's cabin, having to use the brass handrail once or twice as the train jerks from side to side. As you try the door again, however, you suddenly remember that Pierre locked it. So you don't have to bother him again, you kneel down to peep through the keyhole. You can just about see the part of the cabin you want. Were you right about the detail or not? No, you weren't! As you rise to your feet again, you notice Pierre standing behind you, giving a slightly disapproving cough. 'Ah, there you are, Pierre!' you remark with embarrassment. 'I was just checking how good my powers of observation were. *Not* that good, I'm afraid!' ***Go to 21.***

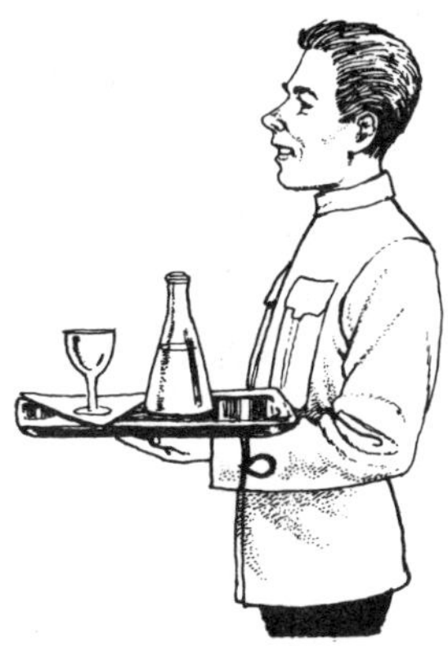

52

Was the top of the oval window in the fatal door the height of Pierre's bow tie, nose or the top of his head?

If you think his bow tie	go to 177
If you think his nose	go to 130
If you think top of his head	go to 228

53

You must be pushing your memory too hard because you suddenly feel rather sleepy! The beautiful scenery passing your cabin window seems to become more and more hazy . . . your eyelids heavier and heavier. Just before you drop off completely, however, you become vaguely aware of a strange smell in the compartment. Then you notice a whitish vapour seeping under the door. It's some sort of gas! Someone's trying to send you to sleep – for ever, probably! You quickly lower the window as far as it will go, then cautiously open the door to see who's lurking in the corridor. But there's just a tiny gas canister there. It looks as if it is nearly empty – but, to make sure, you toss it out of the window!

Record this murder attempt on your COUNTER. Now go to 81.

54

How many drinking-straws were visible?

If you think four	go to 23
If you think five	go to 117
If you think six	go to 168
If you think seven	go to 67

55

You finally reach the Helene carriage and start to read the cabin numbers as you squeeze along the corridor. Arriving at cabin number 7 first, you knock on the door. Suddenly, though, the door of cabin 6 opens instead and the face of Bob Adams pops out. 'I'm afraid Nick isn't there at the moment,' he says, 'but if it's some interviewing you want to be doing, I'm free at the moment. Please come in!' Offering you a toffee from the packet on his seat, he explains, 'I know Nick isn't there at the moment because I heard a key turn in his lock about five minutes ago. I imagine he went for a stroll. He's been very upset by all this business, poor fellow!' You wonder about this, though. If Nick had been for a stroll through the train, how was it that you didn't meet him? But you dismiss this question for a moment and ask Bob how he got on with the director. Did he like or dislike him? 'Oh, dislike – quite definitely,' Bob answers with a laugh. 'I can honestly say he was the most odious

man I ever met!' Appreciating his frankness, you now excuse yourself so you can visit some of the other suspects. You hope you have remembered everything about his cabin correctly.

Throw the SPECIAL DICE – then turn to the appropriate number.

If thrown go to 6

If thrown go to 82

If thrown go to 209

56

Was Giles Blade's right arm on the armrest?

If you think yes	go to 7
If you think no	go to 232

57

When you have finished interviewing those suspects resting in their cabins, you return to your own cabin so you can ring for Pierre again. You want to ask him where you might find the other three suspects. That's quick, you think when, a few seconds later, Pierre knocks on your door. Except it isn't Pierre at all. It's someone in a black ski-mask which covers the whole of the face! And there's a gun in his or her hand. It's obviously the murderer! The sinister-looking figure slowly advances towards you, ready to pull the trigger. You pray that Pierre's footsteps very soon start to echo along the corridor. They might just scare the murderer off!

Record this murder attempt on your COUNTER. Now go to 282. (Remember: when there have been three murder attempts against you, this game is over and you must guess the murderer immediately.)

58

How many glasses were on the bar of the cocktail-car?

If you think two go to 123
If you think three go to 284
If you think four go to 174

59

Shortly after the train has left Zurich, a steward arrives at your cabin. He tells you that he has come to make up the bed. So you don't get in his way while he's doing this, you go for a brief stroll along the train. When you re-enter the cabin some ten minutes later, you find that the bed is all prepared and the steward has gone. Unfortunately, of course, you can't use the bed! At least, not until you have worked out who the murderer is. So, with a rather weary sigh, you sit on the seat beneath the bed, starting to study the notes you have jotted down. What you don't realise, though, is that the murderer had slipped into your cabin after the steward left and had *loosened* the supports holding up the bed. At the train's first big jolt, the whole thing comes crashing down on top of you!

Record this murder attempt on your COUNTER. Now go to 152. (Remember: when there have been three murder attempts against you, this game is over and you must guess who the murderer is immediately.)

60

How many of the two boxes' 'lid-flaps' were visible from the door of the cabin?

If you think four	go to 200
If you think five	go to 244
If you think six	go to 99
If you think seven	go to 260

61

You now decide it's time to meet all the suspects in this case and you ask Pierre where you can find the other members of the film team. 'They're all in the cocktail-car, I believe,' he replies. 'That was Mr Blade's idea. He said that if they all kept together they could make sure that none of them slipped off while the express was in Innsbruck station!' Does that mean that Giles Blade can be eliminated from your suspicions, you wonder, as you now follow Pierre towards the cocktail-car. Not necessarily. Perhaps that suggestion was just a very clever ploy by Mr Blade to show his innocence! As you enter the elegant cocktail-car, passing the curved mahogany bar at one end, you notice that all the suspects are sitting in pairs. You consider which pair to approach first.

If you prefer Bob and Tom	go to 89
If you prefer Iris and Giles	go to 156
If you prefer Jacqui and Nick	go to 230

62

Was the spout of the teapot pointing towards Tom or Jacqui?

If you think Tom	go to 262
If you think Jacqui	go to 131

63

You decide to return to the fatal door! Not only do you want to find out if you were right or not about that detail – but it also occurs to you that the murderer might have left some fingerprints there. If the director had put up a bit of a struggle before he was pushed off, the murderer's hand might have accidentally touched the window. When you closely examine the glass in the door, however, you can see not the slightest trace of fingerprints. Obviously the murderer was wearing gloves. And suddenly a pair of black leather gloves appear at your throat, trying to throttle you! The murderer must have crept up behind you! Fighting for your life, you just manage to prize the hands apart. The murderer quickly disappears into the next carriage, however, before you can turn round to see who it is.

Record this murder attempt on your COUNTER. Now go to 101.

64

How many people on the station were wearing striped woollen hats?

If you think two	go to 39
If you think three	go to 278
If you think four	go to 194

65

Bob and Jacqui obviously notice you watching them from your seat because they suddenly wave in your direction. You wonder if they are as unconcerned by your presence as they pretend. But they both remain exactly as they were, continuing to talk to each other just outside one of the open carriage doors. What a pity you're well out of earshot of their conversation! You can't believe that it is quite as trivial as they are trying to make it look. You wouldn't mind betting

that it's *you* they are really discussing. They're probably both wishing that the train would leave without you! But perhaps you're being unnecessarily suspicious about Bob and Jacqui . . . because they both suddenly beckon you towards the train. They're trying to tell you that it's about to leave. Making sure that all the other suspects have also boarded the train, you quickly step on board yourself. As you make your way back to your cabin to warm up, you try to keep that picture of Bob and Jacqui chatting on the platform firmly in your mind. Did you remember everything correctly?

Throw the SPECIAL DICE to test yourself.

If thrown go to 283
If thrown go to 171
If thrown go to 223

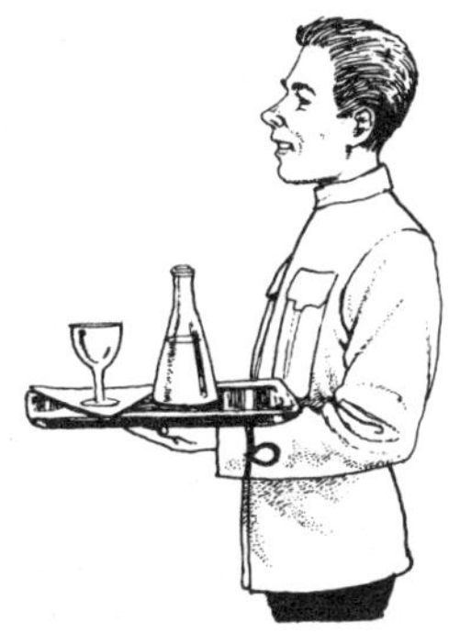

66

How many tied-back curtains were visible in the observation car?

If you think one go to 97
If you think two go to 144
If you think three go to 258
If you think four go to 11

67

Pierre leads you from one carriage to the next, finally stopping at a door with cabin 5 written on it. He leaves you to make yourself comfortable in the lavish compartment, telling you to ring the brass bell near the door should you need him again. After testing the velvet-covered seats, you move over to the window to enjoy the passing scenery for a while. As you are staring out, there's a knock on the door. A white-gloved hand appears round it, placing a small dish of grapes just inside your cabin. 'Thank you,' you call out, assuming this to be one of the cabin waiters. But when you sample a couple of the grapes a few minutes later, you realise that it obviously wasn't a waiter – for the grapes have been laced with poison! You spit them out only just in time!

Record this murder attempt on your COUNTER. Now go to 81.

68

How many brackets were holding up the luggage rack in Iris's cabin?

If you think one	go to 238
If you think two	go to 27
If you think three	go to 272

69

Wandering along to the cocktail-car, you find that, apart from the barman, Tom Henson is the only one in there at the moment. He is leaning on the bar, quietly enjoying a glass of lager. You wonder what he is thinking about. 'Hello there!' he greets you, amiably. 'My turn to be interviewed, is it? Don't look so concerned – I am perfectly sober. This is alcohol-free lager I'm drinking! Now, what is it you would like to ask me? I'll do anything I can to help in your investigations.' Wondering if Tom Henson really is as nice as he makes out, you ask him for a full account of what he was doing at the time Larry Frost was pushed from the train. 'Well, there's not much to tell you really,' he replies. 'Rehearsing my lines in my

cabin – that's all. I can tell you exactly what *scene* I was rehearsing when I heard the terrible news, if you like. But I can't see how that will help you much.' To be honest, you can't either – and so, after thanking Tom for his co-operation, you now leave the cocktail-car. On your way to the observation car to interview Jacqui, you test your memory on what you have just observed.

Throw the SPECIAL DICE – then turn to the appropriate number.

If	[pistol]	thrown	go to 233
If	[dagger]	thrown	go to 165
If	[poison bottle]	thrown	go to 44

70

Which of the brackets holding up the brass handrail in the corridor was beneath the Olympic Express motif?

If you think nearest bracket	go to 123
If you think middle bracket	go to 284
If you think furthest bracket	go to 174

71

When you have finished interviewing those three suspects in the dining-car, you return to your cabin. It means that you have questioned all *six* suspects now and so perhaps you can work out which one is the murderer! When you enter your cabin, you are surprised to find that the window has been lowered right down. Surely it couldn't have been one of the stewards who had done this? It's made your cabin absolutely freezing! It's only when you go to close the window that you realise that it was the *murderer* who had lowered it. And why? To make sure that you stood directly in line with the door, because a gun is suddenly fired at the door from the other side! Fortunately, the bullet just misses you. But will the murderer realise this and fire again . . .

Record this murder attempt on your COUNTER. Now go to 47. (Remember: when there have been three murder attempts against you, this game is over and you must guess who the murderer is immediately.)

72

Which of the drawers in the chocolate machine near Iris and Tom's bench contained the most bars of chocolate?

Drawer nearest Iris and Tom	go to 158
Drawer second nearest Iris and Tom	go to 83
Drawer second furthest away from Iris and Tom	go to 211
Drawer furthest away from Iris and Tom	go to 264

73

You decide to let the suspects have ten minutes or so to settle again on the train before continuing with your interviews. So you return to your cabin, picking up the train's glossy brochure there to find out where your next stop is. The answer is Zurich! After that, the train travels right the way through the night until it reaches Paris early the next morning. So that gives you about ten or eleven hours to work out who the murderer is. If you haven't done it by then, it will be too late! ***Go to 303.***

74

Next to which cabin door was Nick standing when he was talking to you?

If you think number 6	go to 97
If you think number 7	go to 11

75

As Nick and Giles stroll further and further from the train, you wonder where they are heading – it can't bc for either of the station cafeterias because they are both closed. In fact, everywhere on the station is closed. It *is* after midnight, after all. So you begin to become rather concerned about them, wondering if they are intending to stroll right out of the station! But then you notice that there is just *one* place on the station that is still open. A newspaper stand. And, to your relief, you see that this is where Giles and Nick stop. Giles buys a paper at the stand, immediately flicking through

the pages looking for something. You guess that it is tomorrow's weather report because he bad-temperedly shakes his head as he shows that section of the paper to Nick. But Nick seems more concerned about the time, repeatedly glancing at the station clock above them. He anxiously tugs at Giles's sleeve, eventually persuading him to start making his way back to the train. They are the last two to reboard it. As the train now pulls out of Zurich station, you test your memory on what you have just seen at the newspaper stand.

Throw the SPECIAL DICE – then turn to the appropriate number.

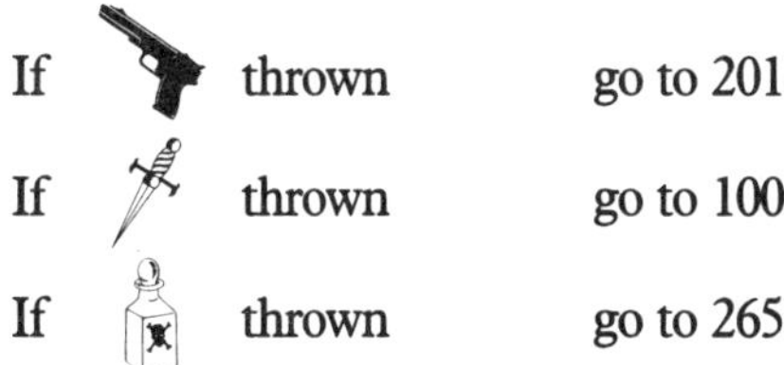

If (pistol) thrown — go to 201
If (dagger) thrown — go to 100
If (poison bottle) thrown — go to 265

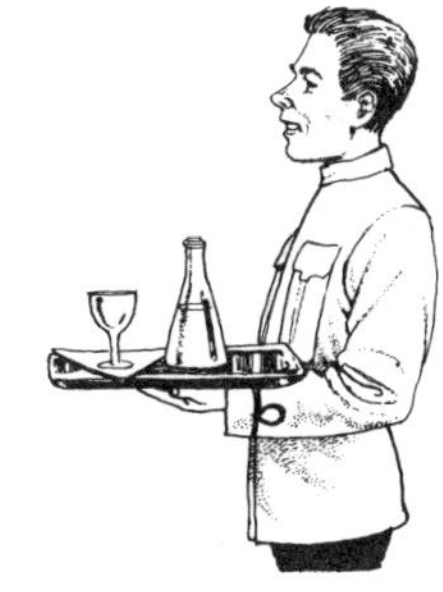

76

Which stack of plastic cups on the refreshment trolley was the highest?

Stack nearest trolley owner	go to 187
Stack furthest from trolley owner	go to 299
Middle stack	go to 31

77

Curious about this shadowy figure, you walk right up to the cabin from where he or she had furtively emerged. The first thing you notice about it is that the lock is broken on the door. Then you notice that there is an upturned suitcase on the seat. Reading the label on the suitcase, you see that it belongs to Larry Frost. Of course . . . this is the cabin that *he* used! That shadowy figure must have been the murderer, sneaking in here to make sure that there wasn't anything incriminating amongst Larry's belongings. Perhaps he or she lured Larry to the fatal carriage door by slipping a note under his cabin door, for instance . . . and perhaps that note had since gone missing! Anyway, the murderer might well regret making this late-night search of the cabin, for you noticed something about them, a small clue, as he or she left!

You may pick up one of the coloured CLUE cards. Placc this exactly over your DETECTIVE'S NOTEBOOK card to 'write down' this clue. Now go to 152.

78

How many ceramic tiles were there behind the basin?

If you think three	go to 244
If you think four	go to 200
If you think five	go to 260
If you think six	go to 99

79

You now start to think about the murder again, resting your head back against the comfortable seat. But as the express reaches full speed once more, gently rocking you, you're sure that it's going to send you to sleep. A little exercise is what you need! So you wander out into the corridor and stroll down the carriage. As you stop at one of the exit doors, hoping to find some inspiration there as to who pushed out Larry Frost, everything suddenly goes dark. Someone has slipped a blindfold over your eyes. Then you feel a rush of cold air as the exit door is thrown wide open. It's obviously the murderer behind you . . . and he or she is now trying to push *you* off the train too!

Record this murder attempt on your COUNTER. Now go to 271. (Remember: when there have been three murder attempts against you, this game is over and you must guess the murderer immediately.)

80

Was Iris holding the handkerchief in her left or right hand?

If you think left	go to 262
If you think right	go to 131

81

Some while later, you notice that the train is slowing down. Looking out of your cabin window, you see that it is because you are arriving at a station. You decide to keep watching at your window just to make sure that none of the suspects furtively leaves the train during its stop. Fortunately, although it's beginning to get dark outside now, the thick snow everywhere means that it is still fairly easy to see. Suddenly, one of the suspects *does* step from the train: Giles Blade! You're just about to run down the corridor after him when you notice all the other suspects stepping on to the platform as well. They're obviously just stretching their legs! You intend to keep a close eye on them, though, just in case. The trouble is they're all moving to different parts of the platform. Jacqui is accompanying Giles to the left end, Bob and Nick are strolling to the right end, and Iris and Tom have just sat down on a bench in the very middle of the platform. Which pair should you watch the most closely?

If you prefer Jacqui and Giles go to 196
If you prefer Bob and Nick go to 5
If you prefer Iris and Tom go to 270

82

How far down had the window blind been pulled in Bob's cabin?

If you think half-way go to 238
If you think third of way go to 27
If you think not at all go to 272

83

Not long after leaving the station, the express starts to cross a very high bridge. As you look down into the snowy valley way, way below, it occurs to you that this must be very like the bridge that the train was crossing when the director was pushed off.

You shiver at the thought! You shiver again because there's a sudden scream from the corridor. You're not sure whether it's a male or female screaming but you dash out into the corridor, convinced that *someone else* has just been pushed out! And, sure enough, there's a wide-open exit door to your left, swinging in the wind! You hurry up to it and peer into the valley far below. It's only then that you realise that the scream belonged to the murderer . . . and it was all to set a trap for you. For he or she suddenly creeps up on you from behind, trying to force you out of the open door!

Record this murder attempt on your COUNTER. Now go to 182.

84

Which item on Jacqui's table was nearest the empty chair opposite her?

If you think salt-pot	go to 305
If you think pepper-pot	go to 71
If you think breadsticks container	go to 164
If you think butter-dish	go to 13

85

As you walk through the dark silent corridors towards the dining-car, you nervously glance over your shoulder once or twice. The train is a lot more eerie now that everyone has retired to bed. And you find the dining-car especially eerie! Peering through the glass of its partition door, you can see nothing but shadows. It's difficult to believe that only a few hours ago the place was humming with conversation and tinkling with cutlery. Tensely, you step inside the dining-car, just able to see someone sitting with his back to you at the very end table. Strangely, he appears to be eating a meal – because there are plates and a wine bottle in front of him. When you edge right up to the table, however, you discover that this person is just a dummy! You guess that it is one of the props for the film,

intended for use in a stunt sequence. There's something else you guess . . . that this is all a practical joke by the murderer! This is confirmed when you hear a faint mocking laughter from the other end of the dining-car. Hearing the person suddenly turn and run, you start to give chase. You hope you have remembered everything about the table correctly in case an important clue was left there!

Throw the SPECIAL DICE to test your memory.

If [gun] thrown go to 189

If [dagger] thrown go to 16

If [poison] thrown go to 215

86

Not long after the train has left Zurich, a steward appears in your cabin to tell you that the staff will soon be finishing for the night. He asks if there is anything else you want before they do. Since there isn't, he wishes you goodnight! As soon as he is gone, you decide that you had better keep your cabin door locked for the rest of the night as a precautionary measure. You don't want the murderer suddenly barging in at three o'clock in the morning! Unfortunately, it doesn't occur to you to ask the steward to lock the empty cabin next door as well. Half an hour or so later, the murderer creeps into this cabin, leaning right out of the window to reach the edge of yours. How do you know this? Because the barrel of a gun suddenly appears at your window, pointing roughly in your direction!

Record this murder attempt on your COUNTER. Now go to 33. (Remember: when there have been three murder attempts against you, this game is over and you must guess the murderer immediately.)

87

You have now reached the fatal door, the one through which the film director was pushed, and Pierre squeezes to one side of the narrow corridor so you can examine it. 'How did you know immediately that it was Mr Frost's shoe that was lying next to the opened door?' you ask him as you test the door's lock to make sure that it's secure. 'You remember me saying that he jumped up angrily from the table?' Pierre obliges with a reply. 'Well, as he did so, he splashed some of the soup on to his shoe. That's when I noticed what type he was wearing!' ***Go to 61.***

88

On which side of Jacqui's plate was her knife?

If you think aisle side	go to 53
If you think window side	go to 192

89

'I know who you are!' Bob Adams welcomes you as you decide to introduce yourself to him and Tom Henson first. 'You're the detective who's come on board to find out which one of us is the

murderer! Let me order you a drink. I can tell you, this has come as such a terrible shock to us both that Tom and I have had a few already!' You kindly accept Bob Adams' offer, asking for an orange juice. While you are sipping it, you tactfully suggest to the two of them that they make this their last alcoholic drink for the time being. 'There's quite a lot of important questions I want to ask you both a little later,' you tell them, 'and I want your answers to be as fair on yourselves as possible!' After giving the same piece of advice to the other two pairs of suspects as well, you ask Pierre if he can make a cabin available to you. You would like a few minutes on your own to think about what you have found out so far. 'Yes, of course,' Pierre answers, starting to lead you down the corridor again as the train jerks from side to side. As you follow him, you test your memory on the details of Bob and Tom's table in the bar . . .

Throw the SPECIAL DICE – then turn to the appropriate number.

If thrown go to 207

If thrown go to 286

If thrown go to 38

90

How many cakes were on the cake stand on Giles and Nick's table?

If you think five go to 262
If you think six go to 178
If you think seven go to 37

91

After you have interviewed each of the three suspects resting in their cabins, you return to your own cabin. As you unlock the door, you notice that a folded sheet of paper has been slipped underneath. Curious, you sit down to read what's inside. It says: 'I'm one of the junior stewards on the train but I don't want to give my name in case it puts my life in danger. I was just stcpping out of one of the empty cabins when I glimpsed someone's back at the other end of the corridor. The person was leaning over the exit door where Mr Frost had been pushed out! I realised that it must be the murderer and quickly jumped back into the empty cabin. Why did I realise that? – because he or she was obviously cleaning fingerprints from the door. I'm sorry I was too frightened to take more in about that person but I did notice the following small detail . . .

You may pick up one of the coloured CLUE cards. Place this exactly over your DETECTIVE'S NOTEBOOK card to find out what this small detail was. Now go to 282.

92

In which direction was the barrel of the gun in Bob's cabin pointing?

Towards Bob	go to 139
Towards reader	go to 41
Towards lamp on table	go to 232
Towards camera on table	go to 7

93

Slowly making your way back to your cabin along the narrow corridors, you suddenly notice that your door is slightly open. Has the murderer slipped inside, you wonder anxiously. You enter your cabin very cautiously, opening the door only fraction by fraction. You are expecting to see someone standing there pointing a gun at you . . . but it's completely empty. You are just breathing a sigh of relief when your feet suddenly slide away from beneath you, causing you to bang your head against the little pull-out table. The murderer obviously *had* been into your cabin after all, for there's a treacherous pool of oil on the cabin floor!

Record this murder attempt on your COUNTER. Now go to 162.

94

How many sections were there to the roof of the Hercules carriage?

If you think three	go to 218
If you think four	go to 73

95

'I hope it won't spoil your meal if I join you for a few minutes,' you say to Nick Todd as you approach his table. He unhappily shakes his head. 'No,' he replies. 'I've lost all my appetite anyway.' He absent-mindedly prods the cheese on his plate with a knife. 'First,' he mumbles, 'I have only a mouthful of soup. Then just a bite or two from the main dish – I can't even remember what it was now!

Salmon, I think. And now all I've had from the cheese platter is the tiniest of slivers. The waiters must think me the fussiest person they've ever served!' You are not sure whether Nick's loss of appetite is because of worry . . . or guilt! 'It seems that everyone in the film team really disliked the director,' you remark as you watch him prodding the cheese again. 'What was *your* reason for disliking him?' Nick takes a while to answer. 'Because he was impossible to

work with,' he eventually replies. He thought all technicians were incompetent. Well, as far as I'm concerned, I was just as good at my job as he was at his!' Thanking Nick for his time, you now move away towards the other suspects in the dining-car. Have you remembered everything about Nick's table correctly, though?

Throw the SPECIAL DICE – then turn to the appropriate number.

If	thrown	go to 173
If	thrown	go to 213
If	thrown	go to 249

96

Which curtain in the observation car wasn't tied back?

Nearest curtain	go to 123
Second nearest curtain	go to 284
Furthest curtain	go to 174

97

A good hour later, you have at last completed your interviews with those remaining three suspects: Tom, Jacqui and Nick. You return to your cabin to think about the answers they gave you. When you open your cabin door, however, you find that the door handle is covered with butter! Surprised that a steward on such an elegant train as this could be so sloppy, you irritably make your way to the washroom up the corridor to clean your hands. Perhaps you should have realised that it *wasn't* a steward who had smeared the butter on your door handle. It was in fact the *murderer*, trying to lure you towards the washroom sink! For when you turn on the taps, a nasty vapour rises from it, making you gasp and choke. The murderer must have sprinkled the sink with some sort of dangerous chemical that reacts with water!

Record this murder attempt on your COUNTER. Now go to 47. (Remember: when there have been three murder attempts against you, this game is over and you must guess who the murderer is immediately.)

98

How many letters were wholly or partly visible on the board at the top of the refreshment trolley?

If you think four	go to 299
If you think five	go to 31
If you think six	go to 187
If you think seven	go to 111

99

You quickly make your way through the train's shadowy corridors after the murderer, hurrying from one carriage to the next. You must be nearing the other end of the train. You smile to yourself as you realise that the murderer will soon be trapped, he or she won't escape you twice! That's surely the very last carriage coming up now and you charge through its connecting door. But you suddenly find yourself in space, a fast cold wind blowing all around you. You've already passed *through* the last carriage . . . this is the exit door right at the very end of the train! As you desperately hang on to the outside of the door, you hear a mocking laugh from the darkness nearby. The murderer must have quickly unbolted this door and then hidden at one side of it to await your arrival!

Record this murder attempt on your COUNTER. Now go to 121.

100

Where were Giles's hands in relation to the paper he was reading?

Above photograph on back page	go to 296
Level with photograph on back page	go to 248
Below photograph on back page	go to 59

101

You are just about to go off in search of Pierre again when he reappears in your carriage. 'That's odd!' he remarks, scratching his head. 'I visited every single cabin in the next carriage but they were all empty. Someone must have rung their cabin bell and immediately crept off somewhere else in the train. I wonder why?' *YOU* know exactly why, however! The person who rang the bell was obviously the murderer . . . wanting to lure Pierre away in order to check what you were up to. If only you had seen who it was! You decide you had better immediately meet all the suspects, asking

Pierre where you can find them. 'They should all be in the dining-car now,' he replies, 'ordering their afternoon tea.' As he leads you towards that carriage, he asks whose table you would like to be taken to first . . .

If you prefer Giles and Tom's	go to 250
If you prefer Iris and Jacqui's	go to 135
If you prefer Bob and Nick's	go to 206

102

How many flowers were in the vase on Bob and Nick's table?

If you think four	go to 192
If you think five	go to 53
If you think six	go to 3

103

After trying every cabin number Pierre gave you, you manage to find three of the suspects in all. And some quite interesting answers you obtain from them as well! You now wonder where on the train the other three suspects are: Tom, Jacqui and Nick. They're either in the dining-car, the cocktail-car, the observation car . . . or deliberately hiding from you in their cabins! Well, there really is little point in them hiding, you think with a smile, as you return to your cabin. Your paths are bound to cross some time. All it means is that they are attracting more suspicion to themselves than they need! ***Go to 282.***

104

How were Iris's legs crossed?

Crossed at ankle, left over right	go to 254
Crossed at ankle, right over left	go to 57
Crossed at knee, left over right	go to 91
Crossed at knee, right over left	go to 160

105

Pierre was right in thinking that Bob Adams was in his cabin at the moment, for when you knock at his door, Bob's friendly voice asks you to step in. But you wonder whether you have caught him in the act because he's adding a few drops of liquid to the middle of a sandwich. And the bottle the liquid has come from is marked 'poison'! 'No need to look so alarmed!' he grins. 'I'm not trying to poison this sandwich for anyone. I intend to eat it myself. This is a

salmon sandwich but they never put enough vinegar on them. So I always carry a little bottle with me!' You're still a little suspicious about the bottle, though, asking why it is marked 'poison'. 'Oh, that's easy to explain,' he laughs. 'This bottle was one of the props for the last murder film I worked on. I decided to keep it as a souvenir! Now what questions do you want to ask me?' You tell him there's only one question – who did *he* think disposed of Larry Frost? 'Well, there's an interesting one!' he says, thinking hard. 'Jacqui Dean would be my bet. She hated him yelling at her all the time!' Thanking him for this information, you now go in search of some of the other suspects. Did you remember everything about Bob's cabin correctly, though?

Throw the SPECIAL DICE – then turn to the appropriate number.

If	thrown	go to 288
If	thrown	go to 231
If	thrown	go to 138

106

Did the coat hanging from the hook in Iris's cabin trail down as far as the flat part of the seat?

If you think yes go to 232
If you think no go to 7

107

You have been back in your cabin for a good ten minutes now but you still haven't properly warmed up again. You're beginning to wish that you hadn't gone for that breath of fresh air on the platform after all! You decide that a hot drink is probably the answer. What sort, though? Then you remember which country you are travelling through now – Switzerland. And what do you associate with Switzerland . . . chocolate! So you decide that's what you will order; a piping hot mug of drinking chocolate! But it's not *just* drinking chocolate that a little later arrives in your cabin. Someone has slipped some poison into your mug as well. Unfortunately, it's not until you have drunk a little of it that you realise!

Record this murder attempt on your COUNTER. Now go to 142.

108

Which item on the counter of the frankfurter stall was nearest the man serving?

If you think vinegar bottle	go to 17
If you think pickled onion jar	go to 148
If you think gherkin jar	go to 86

109

Tensely you slip through the door of the dining-car. You slowly pass the door to the washroom, then the door to the kitchen. Continuing along the dark eerie corridor, you finally reach the luggage-van. It is the very last carriage on the train and so the murderer has no escape! But then nor do you! Your pulse beats faster and faster as you venture into the cage of the luggage-van. Is that the murderer crouching there – or is it just a large suitcase?

Gulp! Is that the murderer's foot you've just tripped over? No, it's only a bag of golf clubs. You assume this belongs to the athletic Tom Henson. The same goes for the two tennis rackets. You wonder if you should investigate some of the suspects' luggage to see if there is any incriminating evidence inside them. But just as

you're about to start, you hear a movement from the washroom behind you. Then a dark figure suddenly leaps out and darts back through the train. As you give chase, you wonder if the murderer suddenly made his move then as a diversion tactic to *stop* you searching the luggage. You hope you have remembered all the details of the luggage-van correctly so you can later tell if anything has been moved.

Throw the SPECIAL DICE – then turn to the appropriate number.

If [gun] thrown go to 149

If [dagger] thrown go to 34

If [poison] thrown go to 50

110

How many glasses were on the part of the bar that was between the two stools?

If you think none	go to 244
If you think one	go to 99
If you think two	go to 260
If you think three	go to 200

111

Waiting until the train is well out of the station, you make a visit to the washroom along the corridor. On returning to your cabin, you are surprised to find a small briefcase on your seat. You wonder whom it belongs to. It certainly isn't yours! The only way to find out seems to be to look inside the case and so you put it on your lap to open it. As you lift the lid, however, dense fumes start to rise from the case. They are obviously poisonous because you start to cough and splutter! Realising that the case must have been put there by the murderer, you hurry over to the window. You only hope you can hurl out the case before the fumes completely overpower you!

Record this murder attempt on your COUNTER. Now go to 224. (Remember: when there have been three murder attempts against you, this game is over and you must guess the murderer immediately.)

112

Did the lead from the lamp run down on the side of the smaller or larger pile of blankets?

If you think smaller	go to 260
If you think larger	go to 200

113

You quickly pop your head out of your compartment, catching Pierre's attention just before he disappears into the next carriage. 'I'm sorry to bother you again so soon, Pierre,' you apologise, 'but I wonder if we might have another look at Mr Frost's cabin. There was a detail there that I would like to check on.' Pierre obligingly leads the way back to the victim's cabin, using his passkey once more. 'Ah, I was wrong about the detail!' you remark with a chuckle as you glance into the compartment. 'Perhaps I'm not quite the clever detective that you were led to believe, Pierre!' ***Go to 21.***

114

Where was Larry Frost's soupspoon?

If you think still in soup-bowl	go to 154
If you think on plate	go to 19
If you think on table	go to 87

115

'Ah, you're the clever-dick detective!' Giles Blade growls at you as you introduce yourself. 'You look a bit young to me, to be honest,' he adds gruffly. 'I would have expected someone a lot older. But I suppose the Austrian police know what they're doing!' You decide that you don't really like Mr Blade but you try not to let this influence your suspicions. You now introduce yourself to his companion, Nick Todd. He seems a lot more likeable – shy and quiet – but you try not to be influenced by that either! 'I wish you luck in your investigations,' Nick tells you rather nervously. 'I hope you catch this wicked murderer as soon as possible!' You now pass

on to the other two tables so you can briefly introduce yourself to the rest of the suspects. 'No questions?' Bob Adams asks with surprise as he helps himself to another cake from the silver stand on his table. 'Not yet,' you say, smiling tantalisingly. 'I wish to return to my cabin first to work out my approach. But don't worry, I shall be speaking to you all again quite soon!' As you leave the dining-car, moving down the narrow swaying corridor, you wonder how observant you had been about Giles and Nick's table . . .

Throw the SPECIAL DICE – then turn to the appropriate number.

If thrown go to 136

If thrown go to 90

If thrown go to 2

116

How many sandwiches were on Giles and Tom's table?

If you think five	go to 53
If you think six	go to 3
If you think seven	go to 192
If you think eight	go to 137

117

'Here we are,' Pierre says as he stops in front of you to unlock a door. 'Cabin 5 – the best on the train! I'll leave you to make yourself comfortable. If there's anything you need, just ring that little bell for one of the stewards.' As you test the comfort of the seats, you start to think about those six suspects you have just met. Which onc is thc murderer? To be honest, none of them appeared particularly guilty or suspicious. But you haven't really asked them anything yet. Once you start putting a few awkward questions to them, you hope it will be a different story! ***Go to 81.***

118

How many objects were there on the ledge beneath the middle section of the mirror?

If you think none	go to 99
If you think one	go to 260
If you think two	go to 244

119

'Come in, please!' Bob Adams calls when, several minutes later, you knock on his cabin door. 'Oh, it's you!' he exclaims. 'You gave me a surprise. I thought it was one of the stewards.' Bob Adams gives *you* a surprise as well for on the little table in front of him sits a gun! 'Oh, don't concern yourself about that!' Bob remarks on noticing your glance at it. 'It's not a real gun. It's just a stage one, a prop. You see, I wanted to get a clever camera angle on it for the film we were making. So I brought the gun into my cabin to try out a few ideas.' You don't know whether to believe Bob's explanation for the gun. Maybe he's lying and it *is* a real one after all! Just in case, you keep half an eye on it as you question him. To your relief,

though, the gun remains where it is. He doesn't suddenly reach out for it at any point! 'Well, thank you,' you remark when you have finally finished your questions. You're not completely relaxed about that gun, though, until you have fully closed the door behind you. You only hope your concern about it didn't make you overlook the rest of the details in Bob's cabin.

Throw the SPECIAL DICE – then turn to the appropriate number.

If thrown go to 92

If thrown go to 159

If thrown go to 197

120

What was the position of the miniature brandy bottle on the table in Giles's cabin?

On Giles's side of glass	go to 41
Directly behind glass	go to 139
Directly in front of glass	go to 7

121

Although you are very tired after all your activity, you still won't allow yourself to doze off. You've only got a few hours left to try and solve this case. But these hours pass much more quickly than you would have wished . . . and it's soon morning. Watching all the suspects file into the dining-car for their breakfast, you desperately wonder which one is the murderer. You're still not sure! Shortly after breakfast has finished, the express enters the suburbs of Paris. It then starts to slow down for the station in Paris. Your journey is over! Since you can't possibly detain any of the suspects without definite proof against them, you despondently watch them leave the train one by one. Feeling very frustrated, you again wonder . . . which one was the murderer.

Since your journey has now finished, you will have to guess this. Check if your guess is correct by placing the black SOLUTION card over your DETECTIVE'S NOTEBOOK card. If you want to play the game again, shuffle all the DETECTIVE'S NOTEBOOK cards and pick another one – then return to paragraph 1.

122

How many letters could you see written on the side of the train's carriages?

If you think three	go to 172
If you think four	go to 93
If you think five	go to 280
If you think six	go to 234

123

You don't finally complete your interviews with the remaining two suspects for another half hour or so. But at last you have questioned everyone! You wearily return to your cabin to think about those answers you have been given. You are so weary, in fact, that you fail to notice that your cabin door has been opened. You also fail to notice that there is a knife point sticking out of the back of your seat! The murderer had secretly embedded it there so that it would stab you when you sat down! Of course, you could choose the *opposite* seat to flop down in. Or will you? . . .

Record this murder attempt on your COUNTER. Now go to 47. (Remember: when there have been three murder attempts against you, this game is over and you must guess the murderer immediately.)

124

Which object was nearest to the rectangular mirror?

If you think make-up brush	go to 260
If you think box of tissues	go to 99
If you think hinged powder compact	go to 244

125

You were right to decide to linger in the corridor because it is not long before Nick Todd comes walking through. He obviously has a lot on his mind, though, because he doesn't see you standing there until he has nearly reached you. 'Oh, it's you!' he stammers,

looking even more anxious than he was before. 'I suppose you were waiting here to interview me, were you? Go on then – but I didn't do it, you know!' You wonder if this nervousness is just an act of Nick's. Perhaps he's a better actor than the *real* actors on the train! You ask him to tell you exactly what he was doing when he heard about Mr Frost's murder. 'Yes, of course,' he replies nervously. 'My hands were very greasy because I had just been repairing some of my sound equipment. So I went to one of the washrooms to clean them. While I was in there, I suddenly heard this loud, panicky voice in the corridor. It was a steward telling someone that he'd just learnt that a person had been pushed off the train!' Thanking Nick for his co-operation, you allow him to continue on his way through the corridor. You hope you have remembered every detail about your encounter correctly.

Throw the SPECIAL DICE to test yourself.

If [gun] thrown go to 30

If [dagger] thrown go to 185

If [poison bottle] thrown go to 74

126

How many breadsticks were in the breadsticks container on Jacqui's table?

If you think three go to 71
If you think four go to 164
If you think five go to 13

127

Aware that your cabin could never offer complete protection from the murderer anyway, you resolve to creep along to that fatal carriage door. So tensely you step out into the quiet, shadowy corridor, checking to your left and right. As softly as you can, you make your way through the next two carriages, finally reaching the precise place of the murder. The fatal door looks even eerier seen at this late time of the night! ***Go to 202.***

128

Continuing to look out at the large station, you're surprised to see all six of the suspects suddenly appear there! They must be intending to stretch their legs before turning in for the night. At least, you *hope* that's all that they're intending! Just to make sure one of them doesn't try and make a run for it, you decide to keep a close eye on them. The task isn't made any easier, though, by the fact that they don't keep together on the platform. But at least they go off in pairs. On which pair should you concentrate your attention?

If you prefer Jacqui and Bob	go to 146
If you prefer Nick and Giles	go to 75
If you prefer Iris and Tom	go to 266

129

Before gripping the handle on the washroom door, you glance at the little brass disc above it. The sign reads *vacant*! To begin with, you think that this means that the murderer can't be in there after all. He or she would surely have locked it! But perhaps this is just a ploy by the murderer to try and make you look elsewhere. So tensely you pull down on the handle, very gradually pushing the door inwards.

The gap grows wider and wider but the little room still appears empty. There can't even be anyone hiding *behind* the door because he or she would be reflected in the large angled mirror above the basin. You're just about to try one of the other doors when you

notice that water is trickling from the cold tap. Does this mean that the murderer *is* behind the door after all, crouched down below the mirror? But then you are suddenly shoved into the washroom from behind, and the murderer makes a run for it down the corridor. As you quickly follow after the sound of footsteps, you hope you were sufficiently observant about the contents of the washroom. If the murderer *had* used it recently, he or she might have left some sort of clue in there!

Throw the SPECIAL DICE to test you were sufficiently observant.

If thrown go to 221

If thrown go to 118

If thrown go to 151

130

Were you right about that detail . . . or were you wrong? It nags at you so much that you decide to return to the fatal door to check. You reach the door and discover that you were *right* about it! As you test the lock once more just to make absolutely sure that Larry Frost didn't fall out by accident, you have this strange feeling of being watched. Is the murderer standing behind you? When you slowly turn your head to check, however, there is no one there. Either it was just your imagination . . . or the murderer quickly stepped into the next carriage! ***Go to 101.***

131

You're just about to return to the dining-car to check whether you were right about the detail when you decide that it probably wasn't that important anyway. So you continue towards your cabin, again being rocked from side to side along the corridor. But it's a good job that you are for there's a sudden hiss through the air from behind you – a knife flying past your ear. If you had been standing still, it would have hit you! It's such a shock that you don't turn round instantly, and by the time you do, the corridor is completely empty. Whoever threw that knife has fled!

Record this murder attempt on your COUNTER. Now go to 81.

132

How many cocktail umbrellas were visible?

If you think two	go to 117
If you think three	go to 67

133

The express hasn't left the station far behind when it enters a very long tunnel. It seems to last for miles and miles, obviously running through a mountain. Suddenly, there's a screeching of brakes, the train coming to an abrupt halt in the tunnel. You quickly jump to your feet! Has the murderer pulled the emergency cord so he can make his escape into the darkness? But then a steward comes to tell you that the sudden braking was because there was a stray goat in the tunnel! To your relief, a few seconds later the express starts to move again. ***Go to 222.***

134

What was the exact position of the grit bucket under the station name sign?

Under the word *St.*	go to 208
Under the first half of the word *Anton*	go to 180
Under the second half of the word *Anton*	go to 252

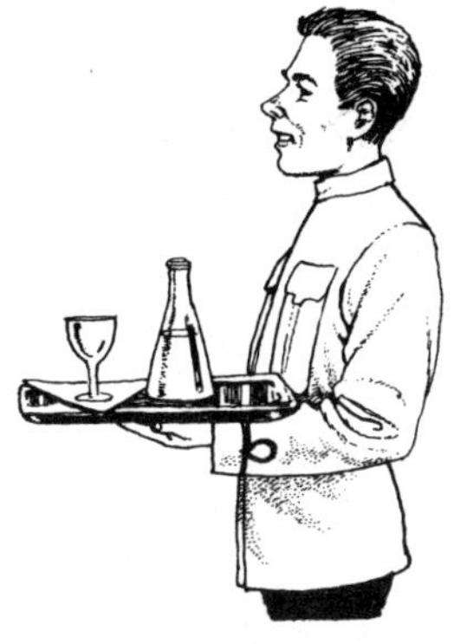

135

As you walk up to Jacqui Dean's table, you hardly recognise her. She doesn't look nearly as attractive as she does in her films. But you assume this is because she has been so shocked by what has happened. Iris Carter also looks very pale. It is to her that you introduce yourself first. 'I know this must be very upsetting for you, Miss Carter,' you begin sympathetically, 'but did you see or hear anything when the director fell from the train?' She replies that she didn't, however, explaining that she was having a short sleep in her compartment at the time. 'And how about you, Miss Dean?' you enquire politely. 'Did you see or hear anything?' Again the answer

is no, however. Jacqui tells you that she was also in her compartment, putting on her make-up for the next scene they were going to shoot. Moving on to the other two tables to introduce yourself there as well, you find that none of the male suspects heard or saw anything either. They too were busy in their compartments. Or, at least, so they claim! You now ask Pierre to show you to your cabin so you can have a think about all these alibis. As you relax by the window, you try to recall the details of Iris and Jacqui's table . . .

Throw the SPECIAL DICE – then turn to the appropriate number.

If thrown go to 277

If thrown go to 179

If thrown go to 88

136

Which object on their table was furthest from Giles?

If you think table number	go to 178
If you think ashtray	go to 262
If you think teapot	go to 37
If you think cake stand	go to 131

137

While you are trying to recall the details about the dining-car, you suddenly notice a tiny silver dish in your cabin. It is on the small wooden table just below the window and contains several delicious-looking chocolates. Written on a card amongst the chocolates are the words: *With the compliments of the Olympic Express*. Unable to resist chocolate, you pop one into your mouth. At first it tastes quite delicious, but then it becomes bitter. It's poison! Fortunately, you didn't swallow and you immediately spit the sweet out before taking a long glass of water. The chocolates came with the compliments of the Olympic Express . . . but the poison with which they had been laced obviously came with the compliments of the murderer!

Record this murder attempt on your COUNTER. Now go to 81.

138

How many sandwiches were on the plate in Bob's cabin?

If you think three	go to 91
If you think four	go to 57

139

After completing your interviews with those three suspects resting in their cabins, you return to your own cabin to think about the answers they gave you. The other three suspects can wait a bit! As you enter your cabin, you notice that a vase of flowers has been placed on the small ledge under the window. Thinking what a nice gesture by Pierre this is, you walk over to breathe in the flowers' scent. As you sniff closely at them, however, you suddenly become very dizzy. Obviously the murderer must have slipped into your cabin and sprayed the flowers with some sort of dangerous chemical. You only hope you can open the window in time!

Record this murder attempt on your COUNTER. Now go to 282. (Remember: when there have been three murder attempts against you, this game is over and you must guess the murderer immediately.)

140

How many objects were on the seat in Giles's cabin?

If you think one	go to 91
If you think two	go to 160
If you think three	go to 254

141

Before resuming your interviews, you decide to let all your suspects settle on the train. So you make your way back to your cabin, intending to relax there for a few minutes. You notice that a glossy magazine has been placed on your table during your absence at the station and you start to leaf through the pages. You have to lick your fingers every so often because some of the pages are slightly stuck together. For some reason, you suddenly start to splutter. Then you realise why. This magazine must have been put here by the murderer – and the pages have obviously been treated with poison! You quickly pour yourself a long glass of water, hoping that you're not too late!

Record this murder attempt on your COUNTER. Now go to 303.

142

You decide you had better find this murderer as quickly as possible. Who knows what he or she will get up to otherwise! You're just about to go looking for the three suspects you haven't yet interviewed, when you remember that dinner is to be served very soon. Perhaps you should delay it until they are all part way through their dinner and feeling more relaxed. They might be less on their guard! So you don't make your way to the dining-car for another twenty minutes. When you *do* finally step in there, you're pleased to see that those three suspects you have still to interview have chosen to dine alone. Who do you want to approach first?

If you prefer Jacqui Dean	go to 29
If you prefer Tom Henson	go to 256
If you prefer Nick Todd	go to 95

143

In which direction was the wine bottle on Tom's table pointing?

Towards window	go to 71
Away from window	go to 164
Towards Tom	go to 13
Away from Tom	go to 305

144

It takes a good hour to find and interview all three remaining suspects – but you at last wearily make your way back to your cabin. You suddenly stop, though, horrified, a shiver running down your spine, for one of the carriage doors is *wide open*, swinging in the fast breeze. It's the very same door where the murder took place! Wondering if the door is now *haunted* in some way, you hurriedly reach out to shut it. But it wasn't Larry Frost's ghost who had opened the door – it was his murderer! As you reach for the door, a silent figure suddenly steps out from the washroom behind you. He or she pushes you hard in the back, trying to make you follow the doomed Larry's path!

Record this murder attempt on your COUNTER. Now go to 47. (Remember: when there have been three murder attempts against you, this game is over and you must guess the murderer immediately.)

145

Was Jacqui's thumb above or below the handrail in the corridor?

If you think above	go to 212
If you think below	go to 284

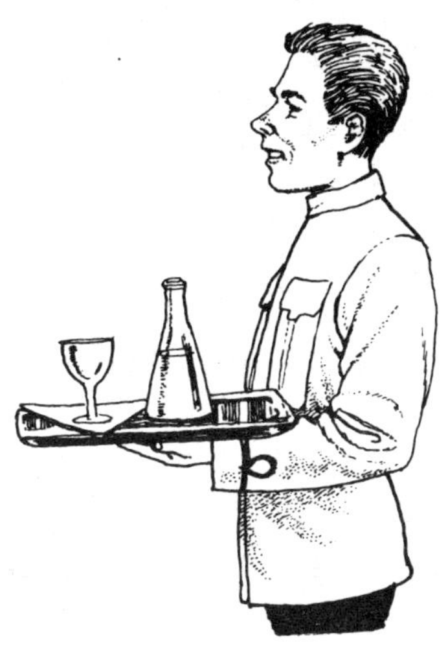

146

You become more and more concerned as you watch Jacqui and Bob. They are strolling further and further away from the train! You're beginning to wonder if they *both* pushed Larry Frost out of the train door . . . and now they're *both* making a run for it! But then you realise that Bob is just leading Jacqui towards a small refreshment trolley. Does he *never* stop eating and drinking? you ask yourself as he buys a cup of coffee. It's little wonder that he's so fat! As he sips his coffee, Jacqui starts to talk to him, pointing back towards the train once or twice. What you would give to be able to hear what she's saying! Perhaps she is telling Bob that she has

worked out who the murderer is and is pointing to his or her cabin! Bob has now finished his coffee and you are relieved to see that the couple start back towards the train. And so do the other four suspects. As the train pulls out of Zurich station a few minutes later, you test your memory on what you have just observed at the refreshment trolley.

Throw the SPECIAL DICE – then turn to the appropriate number.

If thrown go to 98

If thrown go to 76

If thrown go to 259

147

Which of the two mirrors was more upright on the seat?

If you think rectangular mirror	go to 200
If you think oval mirror	go to 260

148

It would appear that everyone on the train retires to bed soon after the express leaves Zurich because it all becomes very quiet outside your cabin. Even the stewards seem to have finished for the night. You would really like to do the same but, of course, you must stay awake until you have *solved* this murder case. You've got a horrible feeling that this will probably mean staying awake right through the night! As the hour grows later and later, you decide to go for a brief stroll along the train to try and wake yourself up a bit. You've just stepped into the silent, rather eerie corridor, however, when all the lights suddenly go out above you. The next thing you know there is a pair of gloved hands at your throat! Will you be able to push these hands off before it's too late?

Record this murder attempt on your COUNTER. Now go to 33. (Remember: when there have been three murder attempts against you, this game is over and you must guess who the murderer is immediately.)

149

How many of the suitcases in the luggage-van had leather straps round them?

If you think two	go to 244
If you think three	go to 99
If you think four	go to 200
If you think five	go to 260

150

You make your way through the dark, silent carriages towards the luggage-van. Reaching it, you squeeze alongside the large cage there. Where's the person you were meant to meet, though? There's no one in sight! You begin to wonder if this is some sort of practical joke (by the murderer, perhaps!) but, just in case it isn't, you decide to wait there a few minutes. While you are waiting, you peer through the cage to look at the luggage inside. You suddenly

spot a pair of black gloves lying on one of the cases. You excitedly wonder if these belong to the murderer, he or she having worn them when actually committing the foul deed! Perhaps they have been hidden here because the murderer was afraid that his or her cabin might be searched. When you step inside the cage to examine the gloves, however, you realise that they are just 'bait' for you, for the murderer suddenly creeps up from behind you and locks the cage! Fortunately, you're quite an expert at picking locks and soon free yourself again. As you now chase after the sound of the murderer's fleeing footsteps, you hope you have remembered everything about the luggage-van correctly.

Throw the SPECIAL DICE to test yourself.

If thrown go to 306
If thrown go to 275
If thrown go to 32

151

How many of the tiles round the back of the basin had ferns painted on them?

If you think three go to 260
If you think four go to 200

152

Retiring to your cabin, you find it very difficult to keep awake as the hour gets later and later. It's now half past two in the morning and you still seem to have got nowhere in unravelling this murder mystery! Again, your head starts to nod . . . but, again, you force your eyes open, deciding to go for a stroll down the corridor to try and wake yourself up. You find the silent shadowy corridor rather eerie, though, and so you soon return to your cabin. You're just starting some vigorous exercises in there, repeatedly touching your toes, when you hear a faint scraping sound behind you. It's the sound of someone slipping a folded note under your door! ***Go to 301.***

153

In which direction was the handle of the wooden spoon pointing?

Towards egg-box	go to 244
Towards broken eggshells	go to 260
Towards flour-bag	go to 99

154

When you have both reached the final carriage door, you start to examine it closely. 'Is there any chance that it could have flown open by accident?' you ask Pierre as you test the handle.

Pierre draws your attention to the lock near the top of the door, however. He shows you how secure it is – and how it can only be opened if someone deliberately *pushes* it open! 'I see what you mean, Pierre,' you comment gravely as he invites you to test the lock yourself. 'So that confirms it. This is definitely a case of murder we are looking at!' ***Go to 61.***

155

How many strands were there to the menu's tassel on Tom and Jacqui's table?

If you think three	go to 131
If you think four	go to 262
If you think five	go to 37
If you think six	go to 178

156

'Champagne!' you exclaim as you stroll up to the table at which Iris and Giles are sitting. 'Is there a cause for celebration, then?' you ask. Giles Blade lifts his cold, hooded eyes to you. No wonder he has taken the part of so many villains over the years, you think – his face is perfect! 'Well, yes, there probably is good cause for celebration, as a matter of fact,' he barks at you. 'Let's be honest, none of us liked that monster of a director. Although I don't see what on earth it has got to do with you!' Remaining polite, you enlighten Giles Blade on exactly what it has to do with you. 'I'm the detective on this case,' you inform him before moving on to the other tables in the bar, 'so I

hope we will be able to talk again later, Mr Blade. And the same goes for you, Miss Carter!' After you have introduced yourself at the tables of the other four suspects, you ask Pierre if he can make a cabin available to you for the rest of the journey. He tells you that this has already been arranged. 'Please come with me,' he requests politely as he leads you out of the bar. While you are following him through the train, you wonder if you have remembered everything about Giles and Iris's table correctly.

Throw the SPECIAL DICE – then turn to the appropriate number.

If	(pistol)	thrown	go to 269
If	(dagger)	thrown	go to 4
If	(poison bottle)	thrown	go to 191

157

Was the teapot nearest Bob or Nick?

If you think Bob	go to 192
If you think Nick	go to 137

158

The express has travelled only a few miles from the station when you are suddenly alarmed by a piercing scream. It seems to be coming from the end of your corridor! Fearing that the murderer is trying to push a second person off the train (perhaps someone who witnessed the first incident), you jump to the door. But when you hurry out into the corridor you find that it is completely empty. Then the 'scream' occurs again – it's just the train's whistle! And a few seconds later, you realise the reason for it. The express is now entering a long tunnel. ***Go to 182.***

159

How many items were on the floor of Bob's cabin?

If you think four	go to 7
If you think five	go to 139
If you think six	go to 41

160

When you have completed your interviews with the three suspects in their cabins, you return to your own cabin. The first thing you notice as you open your cabin door is that the little lamp is missing from the table. The second thing you notice is that yours isn't the only reflection in the window. There's another one moving up behind it! The person had obviously been hiding behind the door! You can't see the person's face very clearly in the reflection – but you *can* clearly see the lamp he or she is holding. It's about to be brought down on your head! Just at that moment, though, the express passes through a crowded station. Will the murderer flee into the corridor to avoid the risk of being seen by anyone on the platform? Or will he just go ahead and strike?

Record this murder attempt on your COUNTER. Now go to 282. (Remember: when there have been three murder attempts against you, this game is over and you must guess the murderer immediately.)

161

How much of the word HERCULES was visible on the side of the Hercules carriage?

If you think *HERC*	go to 218
If you think *HERCU*	go to 73
If you think *HERCUL*	go to 184
If you think *HERCULE*	go to 141

162

You end up taking a much longer rest in your cabin than you originally intended! It's a whole half-hour before you step out of it again and go off in search of the remaining three suspects. Fortunately, you bump into Pierre in the corridor. 'I wish to speak to Jacqui Dean, Tom Henson and Nick Todd now,' you inform him. 'Any ideas where they might be?' Pierre tells you that he last saw Jacqui in the observation car and Tom in the cocktail-car – but he hasn't seen Nick since the train left the last station. 'Perhaps if I linger in the corridor here, he'll come wandering past,' you remark thoughtfully. 'Or shall I simply make my way to either the observation car or the cocktail-car first?' Which will you eventually decide on?

If you prefer observation car	go to 289
If you prefer cocktail-car	go to 69
If you prefer waiting in corridor	go to 125

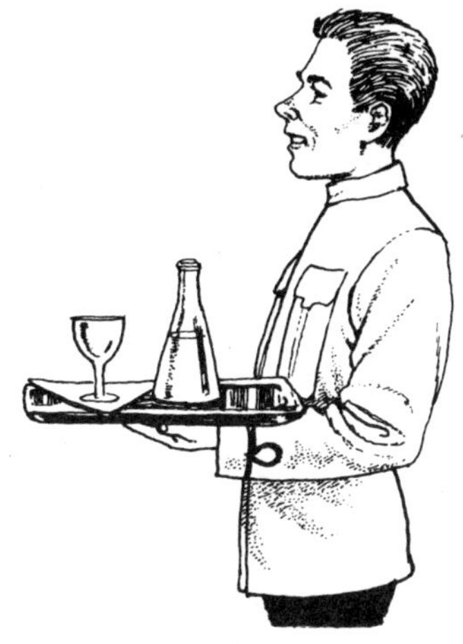

163

There was an ice bucket on the bar of the cocktail-car. Which was nearer to Nick – the main part of this bucket or the lid?

If you think bucket	go to 212
If you think lid	go to 284

164

You've now completed all your interviews in the dining-car and you make your way back towards your cabin to try and come up with some sort of solution to this mystery. You make yourself comfortable by the window, ready to lose yourself in thought. But then you happen to glance up at the luggage-rack opposite. Someone's put a heavy fire-extinguisher up there! You wonder *who* and *why* – but then you suddenly receive an answer to both as the train abruptly screeches to a halt, causing the fire-extinguisher to come flying down towards you. As you desperately try to duck out of the way, you realise that it was the *murderer* who put the extinguisher up there. And that it was the murderer also who just pulled the emergency cord to make the train suddenly brake!

Record this murder attempt on your COUNTER. Now go to 47. (Remember: when there have been three murder attempts against you, this game is over and you must guess the murderer immediately.)

165

How full was the larger of the two bottles behind the bar in the cocktail-car?

If you think a quarter full	go to 11
If you think half-full	go to 258
If you think three-quarters full	go to 144

166

You nervously slip through the end of the dining-car yourself and after a few more steps you arrive at the washroom. You're not sure whether you want to push its door open or not. If the murderer *is* lurking in there, he or she might well be armed! On the other hand, though, the train will be arriving in Paris in a few hours and this is your best opportunity to find out just who the murderer is. So you warily nudge the door open, ready to jump back if there is any movement inside. To your immense relief, you find that the compact washroom is empty . . . but it's obvious that the murderer *had* been in there at some point. And recently! For there's a taunting message scrawled across the mirror. It reads: *YOU'LL NEVER IDENTIFY ME!* You wonder what was used to write

this – then you notice a tube of actor's lipstick to the left of the wash-basin. You are just examining it for fingerprints when the murderer suddenly rushes past the washroom, heading back towards the dining-car and the rest of the train. Again, you didn't quite see who it was! As you hurry back through the train yourself, you hope you have remembered all the details of the washroom correctly.

Throw the SPECIAL DICE to check.

If		thrown	go to 78
If		thrown	go to 225
If		thrown	go to 300

167

How many flowers were in the vase in Larry Frost's cabin?

If you think four	go to 51
If you think five	go to 204
If you think six	go to 298
If you think seven	go to 113

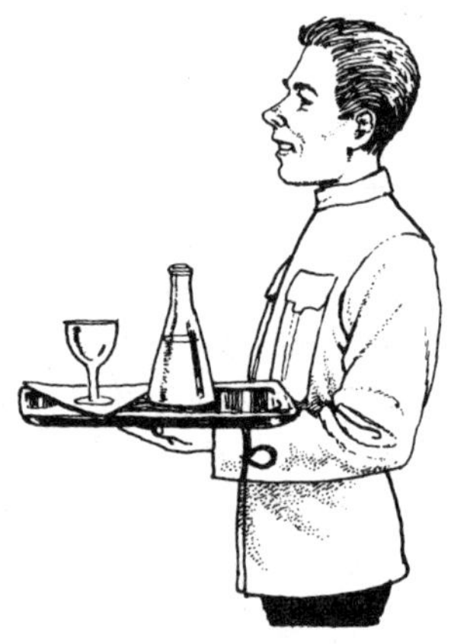

168

Pierre suddenly stops in front of you to unlock a door. 'Feel free to use this cabin for the rest of the journey,' he says as he ushers you into a small, elegant compartment. 'I think you'll find everything to your satisfaction. Ah, I've just noticed the fruit platter! It's empty. I'll just go and fill it for you!' After a couple of minutes, you hear the door softly open again behind you. 'That's most kind of you, Pierre,' you remark over your shoulder without turning round. 'I hope there are some nice grapes on . . .' But the next thing you know, you have been hit over the head with a blunt object. That obviously wasn't Pierre at all but the murderer! You're fortunate that the train rocked a bit just as the murderer struck you or the blow would have been much heavier!

Record this murder attempt on your COUNTER. Now go to 81.

169

How many buckets were on the platform?

If you think one	go to 278
If you think two	go to 133

170

Making your way to the Zeus carriage, you reach Jacqui Dean's door first. But she must be elsewhere in the train because there is no answer to your knock. You have more luck at the next cabin, Iris Carter's. 'I'm sorry to disturb you, Miss Carter,' you tell her as she invites you to step into her compartment, 'but would now be a convenient time to ask you some questions? First of all, I'd like to ask you what you thought of Mr Frost. Did you dislike him for any reason?' Iris seems to consider telling a lie to begin with – but then she decides to be more honest. 'Yes, I did dislike him,' she replies emotionally. 'And there was plenty of reason. He was the most insulting man I ever worked with! But just because I didn't like him,' she insists, starting to cry into a handkerchief, 'doesn't mean I would have pushed him off the train. I know I always play really

nasty parts in my films but I'm not at all like that in real life. It's just acting!' But as you later leave Iris Carter's cabin to search for some of the other suspects, you wonder if those tears of hers are the acting! You also wonder something else – how accurately you have remembered the details of her cabin.

Throw the SPECIAL DICE – then turn to the appropriate number.

If [gun] thrown — go to 195

If [dagger] thrown — go to 68

If [poison] thrown — go to 253

171

Which of Jacqui's feet were completely within the white 'danger' line on the platform?

Just her back foot	go to 107
Both her feet	go to 43
Neither of her feet	go to 198

172

Before doing any more interviewing, you decide to spend a little time in your cabin to warm up. It was absolutely freezing on the platform! Perhaps a bowl of hot soup would help . . . and so you ring the little bell in your cabin for one of the stewards. The soup arrives some ten minutes later and you eagerly dip in your spoon. It needs a little more flavour, though, so you pick up the little pepper-pot that accompanied the soup on the tray, and give it quite a good sprinkle! When you test the soup again, however, you suddenly clutch at your throat. You can taste poison! The murderer has obviously been at work. He or she must have waited until the steward was distracted for a moment and then secretly switched the *real* pepper-pot for a *poisoned* one!

Record this murder attempt on your COUNTER. Now go to 162.

173

Towards which of the following on Nick's table was the flat wedge of cheese pointing?

If you think wine-glass	go to 305
If you think biscuit plate	go to 71
If you think celery sticks	go to 164
If you think grape bowl	go to 13

174

At last your interviews with the remaining suspects – Tom, Nick and Jacqui – are complete, and you make your way back to your cabin. However, you notice that one of the exit doors is wide open! You attempt to shut it again, little realising that this is a trap set for you by the murderer! For just as you reach out to grab the door's handle, the train screeches to an abrupt halt. You are sent hurtling through the doorway and down a steep embankment. The murderer must have secretly watched you approach the door – and then suddenly pulled on the emergency cord!

Record this murder attempt on your COUNTER. Now go to 47. (Remember: when there have been three murder attempts against you, this game is over and you must guess the murderer immediately.)

175

How many bottles were on the two shelves at the back of the bar?

If you think four	go to 99
If you think five	go to 260
If you think six	go to 244

176

'Mr Frost was last seen in the dining-car,' Pierre informs you. 'That was at about two o'clock. He was having a late lunch. If you follow me, I'll take you there.' After walking the length of three carriages, you step into the elegant dining-car. 'Mr Frost was sitting here,' Pierre says, indicating a small table on the right. 'Everything is just as it was. We thought it wise not to touch anything.' You tell Pierre that you would like to speak to the person who was the last to see Larry Frost at the table. Pierre says it was himself. 'Mr Frost had complained to one of the waiters about his soup being cold,' he explains, 'and so I was summoned. I politely pointed out to Mr Frost that that sort of soup was meant to be cold but he just threw

his napkin at me and stormed out. A few minutes later I heard a scream from the adjoining carriage. When I hurried through there, I saw the exit door was wide open and noticed his left shoe lying in the corridor.' As Pierre now leads you along the adjoining carriage to show you this fatal door, you wonder how well you have memorised the particulars of Larry Frost's table.

Throw the SPECIAL DICE to test your memory.

If thrown go to 36

If thrown go to 114

If thrown go to 203

177

You make the short (but wobbly) walk back to the fatal door to see if your memory is reliable. No, it isn't . . . you were wrong about that detail! You are just about to return to the other carriage when the train suddenly jolts, throwing you to the floor. As you slowly rise to your feet again, you notice a small hole in one of the corridor's wooden panels – just above your head. Sure that it wasn't there before, you examine it more closely. There's a bullet embedded in the hole! With horror, you realise what must have happened. Someone obviously fired a gun at you, using a silencer, but fortunately the train jolted at exactly the same time. If it hadn't, that bullet would most certainly have hit you. What an extremely close shave!

Record this muder attempt on your COUNTER. Now go to 101.

178

Returning to the doorway of the dining-car, you find that you were wrong about the detail. 'Are you sure you won't join us for tea?' Tom Henson asks on spotting you there. He waves a hand across his magnificently-laid table. 'There are more than enough sandwiches and cakes for a third!' he smiles. You politely decline his offer, though, telling him that you've decided to have a sandwich sent along to your cabin instead. This means that you can start making some notes about the case while you are eating. The sandwich arrives at your cabin some ten minutes later. It's salmon and cucumber – and looks delicious! After taking a couple of bites of the sandwich, however, you suddenly clutch at your throat. Someone's poisoned it! You quickly down two glasses of water to dilute the poison. A good job you realised in time!

Record this murder attempt on your COUNTER. Now go to 81.

179

Which object on Iris and Jacqui's table was nearest the teapot?

If you think milk jug go to 137
If you think sugar bowl go to 192
If you think Iris's teacup go to 3

180

You return your thoughts to the murder itself, watching the scenery speed faster and faster past your window. 'Which of the six suspects is the evil villain?' you keep asking yourself as the station is now left well behind you. Some refreshment might help your thinking a little – and so you ring your cabin bell for a steward and order a lemonade. The lemonade doesn't arrive for a good quarter of an hour, though. The steward is full of apologies, explaining: 'Everyone on the train seems to be standing in the corridors at the moment. I had trouble squeezing past them all.' It's only when you've drunk some of the lemonade that you realise that one of those people in the corridor must have secretly slipped poison into the glass as the steward squeezed past!

Record this murder attempt on your COUNTER. Now go to 271. (Remember: when there have been three murder attempts against you, this game is over and you must guess the murderer immediately.)

181

In which direction was the clip on Iris's clipboard pointing?

Towards Iris	go to 41
Away from Iris	go to 139
Towards coat on peg	go to 7
Away from coat on peg	go to 232

182

Feeling rather shaken, you decide you had better rest for a few minutes in your cabin. Then you ring the little bell for Pierre. 'Are you all right?' he asks with concern. 'You're looking rather pale.' You assure him that you are OK, though, and add that you think it's about time that you started to interview some of the suspects. 'Whatever you say,' he replies helpfully. 'Might I suggest that you start with Miss Carter, Mr Blade or Mr Adams first? I believe they're all in their cabins at the moment and so it means that you can question them privately.' Agreeing that this is good sense, all you have to do now is decide which of the three to visit first.

If you prefer Iris Carter	go to 9
If you prefer Giles Blade	go to 216
If you prefer Bob Adams	go to 105

183

What was Giles Blade's cabin number?

If you think 2	go to 272
If you think 3	go to 103

184

Returning to your cabin, you notice that a large, yellow box has been put on your seat. There's an orange ribbon round it and a card with the words: *PLEASE ENJOY THIS CAKE WITH OUR COMPLIMENTS*. Assuming that this is from the staff of the Olympic Express, you immediately untie the ribbon and lift off the box lid, only to receive the shock of your life. Inside is a horrible grinning skull! It is not a real skull, of course, but an imitation one – probably one of the props from the film being made on the train. But that doesn't reduce the effect of the shock at all. You gasp for breath, trembling all over. That's obviously just what the murderer intended . . . to scare the life out of you!

Record this murder attempt on your COUNTER. Now go to 303.

185

How many brackets were visible on the brass handrail along the corridor when Nick was talking to you?

If you think one	go to 144
If you think two	go to 258
If you think three	go to 11

186

Jacqui comes walking down your corridor sooner than you could have hoped for – after only three or four minutes, in fact. 'Excuse me, Miss Dean,' you suddenly stop her, popping your head round your cabin door. 'I wonder if now would be a convenient time to ask you a few questions.' Jacqui seems rather irritated by your sudden

appearance, though. You are sure she regrets having come this way! 'Right *now*, you mean?' she asks, almost with a tut at you. 'Must we? I was just making my way to one of the washrooms to check on my hair. It's a real mess from when I got out at the last station!' You promise to limit it to just the one question, therefore.

'Who do *you* think was the murderer?' you ask her. She tosses back that beautiful hair of hers in thought. 'Who do *I* think it was?' she considers. 'Iris Carter, that's who. Iris can be a very spiteful person. I know she's always had it in for me, for instance. Just because I'm a lot more attractive than she is!' Pondering this answer, you now allow Jacqui to continue her stroll towards the washroom. As she disappears down the corridor, you wonder how observant you have been.

Throw the SPECIAL DICE to find out.

If	 [gun]	thrown	go to 304
If	 [dagger]	thrown	go to 70
If	 [poison]	thrown	go to 145

187

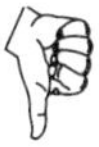

Once the express is well clear of Zurich station, you wander down the corridor so you can use the washroom. When you return to your cabin a few minutes later, you are surprised to see a mug of hot chocolate sitting on your table. Not just surprised – but suspicious! Has one of the stewards thoughtfully put it there for you . . . or was it the murderer? You give the chocolate a cautious sniff to see if it smells of poison. It doesn't, so you take a very tiny sip. You can't *taste* poison either. So, deciding that your suspicion was unfounded, you take a much longer sip of the chocolate. To be honest, it is just what you feel like! Then, as you start to drink from the other side of the mug, you realise how clever the murderer has been. He or she hadn't put the poison in the drink itself – but on part of the mug's rim!

Record this murder attempt on your COUNTER. Now go to 224. (Remember: when there have been three murder attempts against you, this game is over and you must guess the murderer immediately.)

188

Oh no, it's too late – the express is now pulling into the station in Paris! The gentle rocking of the train must have caused you to doze off and you then slept right through the night. But just before the train comes to a stop, one of the platform signs slowly passes your window. To your immense relief, you see that it reads *Zurich*. That means it's only just after midnight. Although you did indeed doze off, obviously it was only for a few minutes. ***Go to 128.***

189

How many items on the menu began with the letter C?

If you think none	go to 244
If you think one	go to 99
If you think two	go to 200
If you think three	go to 260

190

'Ah, you must be the detective we've been hearing about!' Bob Adams exclaims genially as you approach his table. 'A terrible business this, isn't it? Poor Iris here is really upset about it. And I'm a little shaken myself, to tell you the truth. I can't pretend I liked the fellow but I would hardly have wished this on him. Any clues yet?' You politely tell him that that is not something you're prepared to discuss, however, and turn towards Iris Carter. 'Perhaps you should ask the waiter to bring you a little brandy, Miss Carter,' you suggest. 'You look as if you need it!' Iris shakes her head, though. 'No, I'll be all right,' she insists. 'This has all come as a bit of a shock,

that's all. Please find the murderer as soon as you can, won't you? I won't feel safe until you do!' You now move on to the other two tables to introduce yourself to Jacqui and Tom, and to Giles and Nick. You don't interview any of them for the moment, though, deciding to allow them to finish their afternoon tea first. As you squeeze along the corridors back towards your cabin, you wonder if you have remembered all the details about Iris and Bob's table correctly . . .

Throw the SPECIAL DICE – then turn to the appropriate number.

If [pistol] thrown go to 227

If [dagger] thrown go to 205

If [poison bottle] thrown go to 80

191

How were Giles's legs crossed?

Left leg over right leg	go to 23
Right leg over left leg	go to 117

192

Suddenly, there is a knock on your cabin door. A young, apologetic-looking steward appears. 'I'm sorry for disturbing you,' he says, 'but there's something I have to tell you.' You ask him what it is but he refuses to begin until he has stepped right into your cabin and firmly closed the door behind him. Even then, he will only speak in the faintest of whispers . . . ***Go to 291.***

193

How many heaps of swept-up snow were there at the back of the platform?

If you think one	go to 83
If you think two	go to 158
If you think three	go to 211

194

Not long after leaving the station, the express lets out another of its shrill whistles. But this time it is because it is entering a tunnel. It turns out to be a very long tunnel as well, the total darkness outside the window lasting for miles and miles. Suddenly, it goes dark *inside* your cabin as well! You wonder if this is the work of the murderer, your heart beginning to pound. Perhaps he or she has fused your lights somehow from outside . . . and has now quietly slipped into your cabin to deal with you! But your fears are unfounded for the lights suddenly go on again. With a huge sigh of relief you realise that it must have been a brief electrical fault! ***Go to 222.***

195

How many objects were there on the table in Iris's cabin?

If you think three	go to 27
If you think four	go to 238
If you think five	go to 272
If you think six	go to 103

196

As you watch Jacqui and Giles conversing at the left end of the platform, you only wish you could hear what they are actually saying! You consider opening your cabin window but it wouldn't make much difference. The couple are just a bit too far away. So you'll just have to try and guess what they are talking about! You wonder if Jacqui has worked out that Giles must be the murderer – and she is now blackmailing him! Or perhaps it's the other way round? Perhaps Giles *saw* Jacqui push Larry Frost off the train and

is threatening to expose her unless she writes him out a very large cheque. A famous actress like Jacqui Dean would certainly be able to lay her hands on a large amount of money! It's not long, though, before the train emits a loud whistle, shrill in the snow-muffled twilight. It's about to start moving again and all of the suspects quickly reboard it. As the train now pulls out of the station, you test your memory on the part of the platform where Jacqui and Giles had been standing.

Throw the SPECIAL DICE – then turn to the appropriate number.

If	thrown	go to 24
If	thrown	go to 134
If	thrown	go to 267

197

How were Bob's legs crossed?

If you think left over right	go to 7
If you think right over left	go to 232

198

While you are warming yourself up in your cabin, you glance at the brochure with the maroon cover on the little table beneath the window. It tells you all about the history of the Olympic Express and also lists the stations it stops at. You see that your next stop is Zurich, which will be just after midnight. The train then travels right the way through the night, not stopping again until it reaches Paris the following morning. You only hope you have worked out who the murderer is by then. You'll stay up puzzling over it all night if you have to! ***Go to 142.***

199

Did the man serving in the frankfurter stall have an open collar?

If you think no	go to 17
If you think yes	go to 287

200

You quickly pass through the dark corridors after the murderer, the train jerking you to left and right. You can't help bumping into some of the cabin doors. One of those doors is Jacqui Dean's – and another Giles Blade's – and you briefly wonder whether these suspects are *in* their cabins at the moment. Or could it be Giles or Jacqui who is ahead of you, fleeing down the corridor? Perhaps you are about to find out because as you enter the next corridor you glimpse the murderer turn the corner at the end. You start to race down the corridor but then you stop dead in your tracks as a gloved hand suddenly appears round that corner . . . and there is a knife in it. The murderer has lured you into a trap! You quickly turn round, desperately running back to the beginning of the corridor before the knife is thrown . . .

Record this murder attempt on your COUNTER. Now go to 121.

201

How many UPRIGHT newspapers and magazines were on the newspaper stand?

If you think six	go to 248
If you think eight	go to 296
If you think ten	go to 59
If you think twelve	go to 220

202

You are carefully examining the fatal door for fingerprints when you sense that someone is watching you from the shadows at the far end of the corridor. Nervously lifting your head, you are just in time to see a dark figure hurriedly disappear into one of the three doors there. It was either the door to cabin 1, cabin 2, or the washroom. But which? The only way to find out is to walk along there and investigate. As you tensely approach these three doors, you wonder which you should open first.

If you prefer cabin 1	go to 49
If you prefer cabin 2	go to 276
If you prefer washroom	go to 129

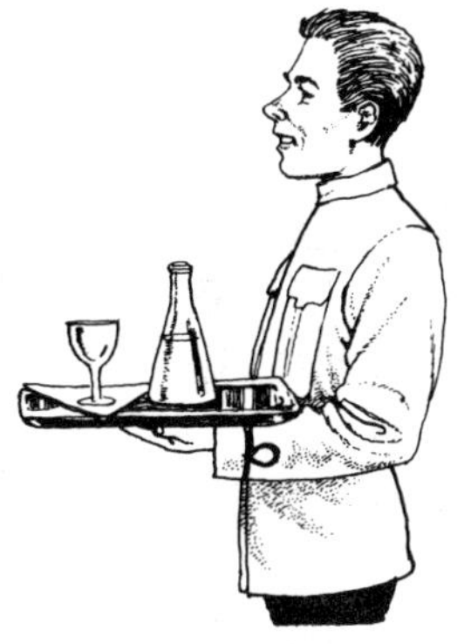

203

Was the curtain at Larry Frost's table tied back?

If you think yes	go to 19
If you think no	go to 268

204

Curious to know whether you were correct about the detail in Larry Frost's cabin, you make your way back there. Opening the door, you glance briefly inside. You were *wrong* – you must try to be more observant next time! You're just pulling the door shut again when something occurs to you. Why was it unlocked? You are sure Pierre had locked it before you left last time. Here's your chance to check because you notice Pierre coming towards you again along the corridor. 'Yes, I thought I'd locked it too,' he replies to your enquiry with a shiver. 'It must mean that someone has picked the lock to snoop round. The murderer, perhaps? Maybe he or she wanted to make sure that Mr Frost hadn't written down any suspicions he might have had!' ***Go to 21.***

205

How many sandwiches were on the sandwich platter on Iris and Bob's table?

If you think three	go to 37
If you think four	go to 178
If you think five	go to 262

206

Introducing yourself at Bob and Nick's table, you watch for a guilty look from either of them. A look that would suggest that *he* was the person who had crept up behind you in the corridor. But although Nick Todd looks rather shy, he certainly doesn't look guilty. And nor does Bob Adams. 'Do you mind if I ask you both how long you have been sitting here?' you ask. Bob Adams lets out a hearty laugh, remarking what a strange question that is. 'I thought you would be more likely to ask what we were doing a couple of hours ago, when Larry Frost was actually pushed from the train!' he comments.

'But you're the boss,' he adds with a shrug. 'Now let me think. I'd say we've both been sitting here for some three or four minutes.' Moving along to the other two tables, you ask the same question there as well. These suspects, also, admit that they have been in the dining-car for just a few minutes. So it could have been any one of the six who had crept up behind you in the corridor! You now ask Pierre to show you to your private cabin. As you make yourself comfortable in this small but elegant compartment, you try to remind yourself of the details of Bob and Nick's table . . .

Throw the SPECIAL DICE – then turn to the appropriate number.

If thrown go to 251

If thrown go to 102

If thrown go to 157

207

Which bottle had least wine in it?

Red wine bottle on table	go to 117
White wine bottle on table	go to 23
Slim bottle on bar	go to 168
Squat bottle on bar	go to 67

208

As the train reaches full speed again, you notice how hot it is in your compartment. Pierre must have turned the heater control far too high. You switch the control down a little and lower the window. 'That's better!' you exclaim as you poke your head right out of the window and breathe in the fresh mountain air. But suddenly the window is yanked up again, trapping your neck! The murderer has crept up behind you and is trying to throttle you! Fortunately, the mysterious person soon flees your compartment, but you are left spluttering badly. Will you recover from this murder attempt?

Record this murder attempt on your COUNTER. Now go to 271. (Remember: when there have been three murder attempts against you, this game is over and you must guess who the murderer is immediately.)

209

What letters were embroidered on the seat's headrest covers in Bob's cabin?

If you think O.E.	go to 272
If you think H.C.	go to 103

210

Iris's cabin is in the Zeus carriage, round about the middle of the train. She quietly invites you in as you knock on her door. 'Oh!' she exclaims, nervously twiddling her fingers. 'I thought it was the warm milk I ordered to try and settle my nerves. You want to speak to me already, do you? I hope that doesn't mean that you think that *I* am the main suspect? It wasn't *me* who pushed Lawrence off the train, I swear to you!' You gently tell Iris to calm down, though, explaining that it was just chance that you chose to interview her first. 'So you swear that it wasn't *you* who pushed the director off the

train?' you begin. 'Then who do you think it was? Do you have any ideas, by any chance?' Iris thinks for a while, starting to fiddle with her fingers again. 'Well, I didn't actually *see* anything, if that's what you mean,' she replies hesitantly. 'But I certainly have my suspicions. My guess is that it's Tom Henson. Poor Tom was worried stiff that Lawrence would wreck his chance of becoming the world's number one star.' You thank Iris for her opinion and go in search of those other two suspects. You hope you have remembered everything about her cabin correctly.

Throw the SPECIAL DICE – then turn to the appropriate number.

If thrown go to 181

If thrown go to 255

If thrown go to 106

211

You've travelled quite a few miles from the station when you hear an occasional banging coming from the corridor. It sounds as if someone hasn't shut one of the exit doors properly. Or perhaps someone has just opened one! Perhaps it was the murderer and he or she has pushed off a second person! So you step out into the corridor to check. Yes, it is an open door – and you dash down the corridor towards it. Only too late do you realise that this was a trap set for you by the murderer . . . because you are suddenly sent flying and bang your head badly on the brass handrail. He or she must have fastened a trip-wire across the corridor!

Record this murder attempt on your COUNTER. Now go to 182.

212

It takes another hour or so to complete your interviews with those remaining three suspects but, at last, you make your way back to your cabin. As you are swaying along one of the corridors, something suddenly strikes the brass handrail at your side. You realise that it was a bullet – and it only just missed you! The murderer is obviously just behind you! You don't have time to turn round and see who it is, though, because you know at any moment now he or she is likely to fire again. You *must* reach the end of the corridor, for you will only be safe when you have turned that corner. So you start to run for all you are worth, praying that you will make it in time . . .

Record this murder attempt on your COUNTER. Now go to 47. (Remember: when there have been three murder attempts against you, this game is over and you must guess the murderer immediately.)

213

How many flowers were in the vase on Nick's table?

If you think three	go to 164
If you think four	go to 71
If you think five	go to 13

214

You read in Larry's diary that he suspected that one of the film team was trying to bump him off. For he writes that several 'accidents' had happened to him over the last couple of days. He states that during one of these 'accidents', he actually got a glimpse of the person who had arranged it. You excitedly read on to find out what Larry has to say about him or her!

You may pick up one of the coloured CLUE cards. Place this exactly over your DETECTIVE'S NOTEBOOK card to find out what Larry noticed about the murderer. Now go to 33.

215

One odd fact about the table was that it was laid for dinner but it wasn't a dinner menu. What type of menu was it?

If you think breakfast	go to 260
If you think lunch	go to 200

216

'Come in!' Giles Blade snaps as you knock on his cabin door. But, on opening the door, you immediately step back into the corridor. He has a dagger in his hand! 'Don't be so ridiculous!' he laughs unpleasantly at you. 'This is just one of my props for the film. I play the murderer!' As you cautiously re-enter Giles's cabin, you ask him exactly what he was doing with the dagger. 'Well, what does it look like?' he snaps. 'Just rehearsing the murder scene, of course. Surely, you're not so stupid as to think I was intending to use it for real!' You're not sure that you are convinced by Giles's explanation for toying with the dagger, however. And you let him know this. 'But what's the point in rehearsing for the film *now*?' you ask him.

'Surely, with its director gone, the film will be abandoned?' Giles reluctantly nods his head in agreement. 'Yes, you're probably right,' he admits. 'That fact hasn't really sunk in yet. It's a great shame. This was one of the best parts I've ever been given!' After a few more questions, you leave Giles's cabin. As you close his door, you hope you have remembered everything you saw there correctly.

Throw the SPECIAL DICE – then turn to the appropriate number.

If thrown go to 42

If thrown go to 140

If thrown go to 279

217

Which hand was Iris holding behind her back as she stood beside the train?

If you think right hand	go to 280
If you think left hand	go to 93

218

As you step back into your cabin again, you discover something rather odd. In fact, *two* rather odd things. Firstly, the table lamp has gone missing from your little table. And, secondly, a strange raincoat has suddenly appeared up in your luggage-rack! Intrigued by this, you reach up to pull the raincoat down. Perhaps the owner's name is embroidered on it somewhere. Tugging at the loose sleeve of the raincoat, though, you suddenly bring down something heavy on your head. So that's where the missing lamp had got to! The murderer had set a nasty trap for you!

Record this murder attempt on your COUNTER. Now go to 303.

219

What object on the drinks table in the observation car was nearest to Jacqui?

Bowl of peanuts	go to 258
Straw in cocktail glass	go to 11
Cocktail stick in cocktail glass	go to 144

220

A steward appears at your door soon after the express has left Zurich, offering to make up the bed in your cabin. Although you don't have any use for a bed just yet (you daren't allow yourself any sleep until you have *cracked* this murder mystery!), you invite the steward in. So you don't get in his way, you go for a brief stroll along the train. By the time you have returned, everything is finished – the upper part of the seat has been pulled up and out, converted into a very inviting bed! You are sorely tempted to test it for a few minutes. What you don't realise, though, is that the murderer slipped into your cabin after the steward left and embedded a knife blade in the mattress, craftily concealing it under the sheets. If you *do* flop on to the bed, it could be very nasty for you. Will you succumb to its invitation or not?

Record this murder attempt on your COUNTER. Now go to 152. (Remember: when there have been three murder attempts against you, this game is over and you must guess the murderer immediately.)

221

Which of the following was nearest to the basin's plug?

Towel-rail	go to 200
One of taps	go to 244
Vase of flowers	go to 99
Bar of soap	go to 260

222

You decide it's about time you started questioning some of the suspects. So you stroll along the corridors towards Pierre's office near the front of the train. You ask him where you are most likely to find the other passengers. 'Well, if you want Miss Dean, Mr Henson or Mr Todd,' he answers, 'I suggest you try the observation car. A steward has just taken a coffee order from them all there. But if you want the other three, I suggest you try their cabins.' Since you would really like to speak to each of the suspects on their own, you decide to go to the cabins first. After Pierre has jotted down the appropriate numbers for you, you consider which cabin to start with . . .

If you decide on Iris's	go to 210
If you decide on Giles's	go to 25
If you decide on Bob's	go to 119

223

Was the steward standing in the doorway of the train holding an oval or rectangular tray?

If you think oval	go to 198
If you think rectangular	go to 274

224

It's the middle of the night now (half past two in the morning) and how you wish you could snuggle up in the bed that a steward has prepared for you in your cabin! But, of course, you can't. You can't drop off to sleep until you have worked out who the murderer is. You are sitting on the edge of the bed, desperately considering all the possibilities, when you hear a muffled voice from the corridor. 'You'll never identify me!' it softly mocks at your door. Of course, by the time you have opened the door, the culprit had disappeared down the corridor. You are sure the footsteps hurry off to the left, though, and so you start to walk that direction yourself . . . ***Go to 242.***

225

How far down did the basin plug hang?

Above empty towel-rail	go to 260
Level with empty towel-rail	go to 244
Below empty towel-rail	go to 99

226

'Hello, you must be Jacqui Dean and Tom Henson,' you say politely as you walk up to the first table. You then introduce yourself. 'I'm the private detective appointed to investigate this murder case,' you explain. You notice that Jacqui's hand is shaking as she sips her tea. Her attractive face looks quite distraught. 'Who would do such a thing?' she wails, running her fingers through her beautiful hair. 'I know none of us really liked Lawrence but I didn't think anyone would go as far as that!' Tom Henson nods his head in agreement. 'Neither did I,' he remarks with disbelief. 'OK,' he adds, 'he kept threatening everyone that they would never work again. But that's hardly reason for pushing the poor man off the

train!' You wonder if Jacqui and Tom are quite as sincere as they sound. You must remember that they are both actors! Perhaps a few searching questions from you would find out how sincere they *really* are. But you decide to leave these for later. It only seems fair to let them finish their afternoon tea first . . . and so you withdraw from the dining-car. As you're making your way back to your compartment you try to remember something about their table . . .

Throw the SPECIAL DICE – then turn to the appropriate number.

If (pistol) thrown go to 155

If (dagger) thrown go to 292

If (poison bottle) thrown go to 62

227

Was the handle on Bob's teacup pointing towards him, towards Iris, towards the window or towards the reader?

If you think towards Bob	go to 178
If you think towards Iris	go to 37
If you think towards window	go to 131
If you think towards reader	go to 262

228

Curious to know whether you were right or not about that detail, you make the short walk back to the fatal door. It turns out that you were wrong! While you are there, though, it suddenly occurs to you that the murderer might have left some fingerprints on the window. In the struggle, the murderer's hand could have momentarily touched the glass. It's a possibility . . . and so you put your face right up to the glass and breathe on it. You're just about to study the condensation that your breath has made when a gloved hand suddenly grabs you from behind. The next thing you know, the gloved hand has opened the door and is trying to push you out. It's the murderer! You desperately hang on, though, and eventually the murderer gives up. He or she hurries off into the next carriage before you have time to turn round and see who it is.

Record this murder attempt on your COUNTER. Now go to 101.

229

How far down was the window blind drawn in Larry Frost's cabin?

If you think a third down	go to 298
If you think half-way down	go to 113

230

As you stroll up to Jacqui and Nick's table, you notice that they are both drinking cocktails! You know this is called the *cocktail*-car but you would have thought something a little more solemn might have been appropriate under the circumstances. A stiff brandy each, for instance! 'I know what you're thinking,' Jacqui Dean remarks as

she catches your glance. 'Fancy drinking colourful cocktails at a time like this. Well, brandy doesn't agree with me, I'm afraid. And as for poor Nick here, I don't think he cares what he drinks as long as it's something to calm his nerves!' You're still not totally convinced by Jacqui's excuses, though. After all, surely there isn't a need to have cheerful-looking paper umbrellas in the cocktails as well! After introducing yourself to the other suspects in the cocktail-car, you ask Pierre if he can make a cabin available to you for the rest of the journey. 'Of course, feel free to use cabin 5,' he says, asking you to follow him through the train so he can unlock it for you. As you are swaying down the corridors, you wonder if you have remembered everything about Jacqui and Nick's table correctly . . .

Test your memory by throwing the SPECIAL DICE.

If	thrown	go to 54
If	thrown	go to 281
If	thrown	go to 132

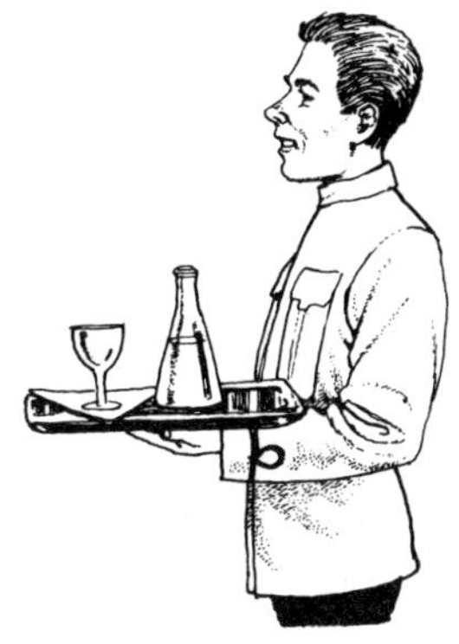

231

What was Bob's cabin number?

If you think 5 go to 160
If you think 6 go to 91
If you think 7 go to 254

232

When you have finished interviewing those three suspects resting in their cabins, you make your way back towards your own cabin to have a think about the answers they gave. As you approach your door, however, you notice that it is slightly ajar! Is someone snooping round inside your cabin? Could the murderer be lying in wait for you? You enter your cabin very warily, fraction by fraction. You're so concerned about what might be *behind* the door, however, that you fail to notice what's *above* the door. A heavy suitcase has been balanced up there! Just as you're thinking that the cabin is perfectly safe, the case falls on top of you as you push the door right open!

Record this murder attempt on your COUNTER. Now go to 282. (Remember: when there have been three murder attempts against you, this game is over and you must guess the murderer immediately.)

233

How many glasses were visible in the cocktail-car?

If you think five — go to 258
If you think six — go to 11
If you think seven — go to 97
If you think eight — go to 144

234

Making your way back to your cabin for a quick warm-up after being out on the platform, you notice that the heater has been switched off. You wonder why one of the stewards has done that. It's colder in here than it is outside, you think, as you turn the control right up. However, you soon realise that it *wasn't* one of the stewards who interfered with your heater; it was the murderer! For unpleasant-smelling fumes soon start to blow from it. The murderer had obviously put some sort of deadly chemical in there which would be activated when the heater was switched on! Coughing and spluttering, you desperately make your way over to the window. You only hope that you will be able to open it in time!

Record this murder attempt on your COUNTER. Now go to 162.

235

Which of the words below was NOT written on the front of the frankfurter stall?

If you think *FRANKFURTERS*	go to 287
If you think *BIER*	go to 86
If you think *HOT-DOGS*	go to 148
If you think *HAMBURGERS*	go to 17

236

As you pass through the dark, silent corridors towards the cocktail-car, you start to grow suspicious about that note. Why didn't the writer just come into your cabin to tell you his information? Perhaps he was worried that someone might see him . . . but who was there to see him at this time of the night, anyway? By the time you reach the cocktail-car you've become quite tense. You nervously peer into the shadows, trying to see if anyone's there. The bar and tables look really eerie now that they are deserted and in darkness. You warily approach the bar, constantly looking over your shoulder. Suddenly you spot someone there, standing amongst the bottles. But then you realise that it's just your reflection in the large mirror

behind the bar. Your next fright, though, is a real one. You hear a scraping sound from the far end of the bar, as if someone has just picked up a bottle. You quickly swing round – it must be the murderer intending to creep up on you! But the shadowy figure flees through the door. As you give chase, you hope you have remembered the details of the bar correctly. The murderer might have accidentally left a clue there!

Throw the SPECIAL DICE to test your memory.

If thrown go to 110

If thrown go to 175

If thrown go to 14

237

Where did the cord on the window blind hang in Iris's cabin?

To left of lampshade	go to 160
To right of lampshade	go to 91
Directly over lampshade	go to 254

238

Well, your search for the suspects was reasonably successful. You managed to find three of them in their cabins in all. The other three – Jacqui, Nick and Tom – were either in one of the corridor washrooms or deliberately hiding from you! However, you don't let this bother you. As long as you keep a watchful eye every time you stop at a station, there's nowhere they can go. You're bound to bump into them on the train some time! So you return to your own cabin for the moment to consider the answers of those three suspects you did speak to: Iris, Giles and Bob. Was one of those the murderer? Although you're far from being absolutely sure yet, you're beginning to have one or two theories! ***Go to 282.***

239

How many flower-baskets were hanging down from the station roof?

If you think none	go to 39
If you think one	go to 194
If you think two	go to 278
If you think three	go to 133

240

You decide to concentrate your attention on Tom and Nick because you notice that Tom has brought out a suitcase with him. Is he intending to make a run for it? Although he remains by the carriage door for the moment, he glances along the platform once or twice. It looks as if he is waiting until the coast is clear! But then you

discover the *real* reason Tom has brought out his suitcase. A customs official walks up to him and kneels down to check the suitcase's contents. The official must have earlier *instructed* Tom to bring it out. It seems that the contents of Tom's suitcase are perfectly in order because the customs official now ticks the clipboard he is carrying and continues along the platform. So at least there aren't any guns, daggers or poison bottles in his case!

You wonder if that means Tom definitely *isn't* the murderer. Not necessarily. He might have those sort of weapons cleverly hidden in his cabin somewhere! Tom now returns to his cabin . . . and so do all the other suspects because the express lets out a long whistle to show that it is ready to leave the station. As you step on to the train yourself, you hope you have remembered everything you saw.

Throw the SPECIAL DICE to test yourself.

If (gun) thrown — go to 161
If (dagger) thrown — go to 10
If (poison bottle) thrown — go to 94

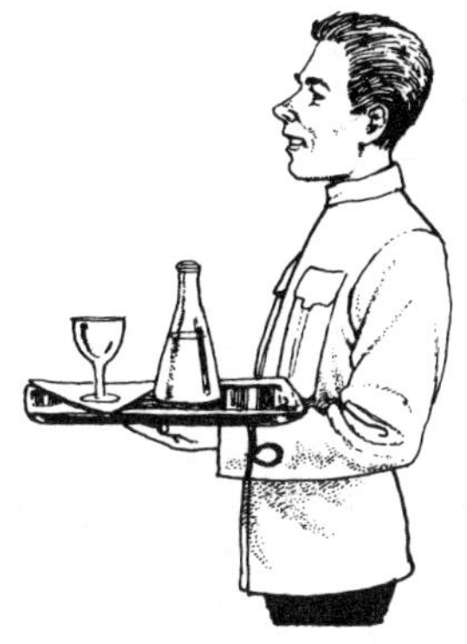

241

Was Tom resting his left or right arm on the chair's armrest?

If you think left — go to 212
If you think right — go to 284

242

You tremble a little as you walk along the quiet, shadowy corridor. You and the murderer seem to be the only two still up. Even the stewards seem to have retired to their cabins now. As you are passing from one silent carriage to the next, you suddenly think you spot the murderer over your shoulder. But it's your own dim reflection in the darkened windows. With heart pounding away, you continue down the corridors, reaching the empty dining-car. As you pass the eerie deserted tables, you hear some cutlery tinkle ahead of you. Nervously lifting your head, you just glimpse a dark figure slipping through the end door. There are only *three* places the murderer can go to now: the dining-car's washroom . . . the kitchen-car . . . and the luggage-van. You anxiously decide which one you should explore first.

If you prefer washroom	go to 166
If you prefer kitchen	go to 15
If you prefer luggage-van	go to 109

243

Were the arms of the ticket collector on the platform in front of him or behind his back?

If you think in front of him	go to 264
If you think behind his back	go to 158

244

Racing down one dark corridor to the next, you are sure you are gaining on the murderer. You are certainly not *loosing* any ground – you can still hear those frantic footsteps. They sound only about a carriage ahead of you now. You hurtle into another corridor, just glimpsing a shadowy figure disappearing through the other end. You so very nearly *saw* the person that time! You are convinced that you will in the very next carriage. So you excitedly charge through the connecting doors! You suddenly crash heavily to the floor, however, sliding half-way along the corridor on your back. The murderer had laid a fire-extinguisher treacherously across your path!

Record this murder attempt on your COUNTER. Now go to 121.

245

How many safety bars were across the window on the fatal door?

If you think two	go to 228
If you think three	go to 177
If you think four	go to 130
If you think five	go to 63

246

You make your way to the Hercules carriage, walking along the dark, swaying corridors. 'Mr Henson!' you call out as you knock on the door of cabin number 1. 'Mr Henson, are you in?' But Tom Henson *isn't* inside – or if he is, he's pretending not to be! So you knock on the door of the adjoining cabin, the one belonging to Giles Blade. 'Who is it?' his abrupt voice calls back. 'Oh, it's you, the clever-dick detective!' he remarks sarcastically as you open his door. 'Well? What is it you want to ask me? Was it me who pushed that obnoxious director off the train? No, it wasn't, as a matter of fact!' You can't resist pointing out to him that even if he wasn't the one who pushed Mr Frost off the train, he doesn't sound that upset about it! 'All right, I couldn't abide the man,' he admits. 'I make no secret about that. But if you think that gives me a good motive then it also gives every other member of the film team a good motive.

They all despised him as well!' You can't help privately agreeing with this logic because you had already perceived that about the other suspects yourself. As you now go in search of some of these, you hope that you have remembered everything about Giles Blade's cabin correctly . . .

Throw the SPECIAL DICE – then turn to the appropriate number.

If		thrown	go to 293
If		thrown	go to 40
If		thrown	go to 183

247

How full was the glass of red wine on Jacqui's table?

More than half-full	go to 13
Less than half-full	go to 305

248

Everyone seems to retire to bed immediately after the train leaves Zurich because the corridors are soon deathly quiet. You wish that you could go to bed yourself but of course you can't until you have worked out who the murderer is. While you're studying the notes you have jotted down so far, you think you hear footsteps in the corridor. Perhaps someone else is still up and about after all. Then you realise that the noise is actually a door banging. Curious, you step out of your cabin and you see that it is the exit door at the far end of your corridor. You stroll along there to shut it but just as you reach out for the handle, you slip on the floor. As you desperately hang on to the door, your legs dangling only centimetres from the fast-moving ground, you realise that what you slipped on was butter. And that it was almost certainly smeared there for you by the murderer!

Record this murder attempt on your COUNTER. Now go to 152. (Remember: when there have been three murder attempts against you, this game is over and you must guess who the murderer is immediately.)

249

Which arm was Nick leaning on?

If you think his right go to 13
If you think his left go to 305

250

As you approach Giles and Tom's table, you wonder if it was either of them who came up behind you while you were investigating the fatal door. They both look perfectly innocent, though; Giles Blade pouring himself a cup of tea and Tom Henson spreading a little

mustard on his ham sandwich. After you have introduced yourself to the two men, you ask them how long they have been sitting there. 'Well, I'm not sure how relevant *that* is to the murder inquiry!' Giles Blade replies rather gruffly. 'But if you must know, I've been here about five minutes and Tom joined me about two minutes ago. Why do you ask?' You avoid his question, though, telling him that you now want to meet the rest of the film crew. When you have briefly introduced yourself to them all, you ask Pierre if he could show you to your cabin. As you make yourself comfortable in this lavish compartment, your thoughts go back to Tom and Giles. You're sure Tom raised an eyebrow when Giles said he had been there for five minutes. Did this mean that Giles was lying? You try to remember what their table looked like – whether it suggested that they had only just sat down.

Throw the SPECIAL DICE – then turn to the appropriate number.

If		thrown	go to 116
If		thrown	go to 22
If		thrown	go to 297

251

Which object on the table was furthest away from Nick?

If you think teapot	go to 53
If you think sandwich platter	go to 137
If you think cake stand	go to 192
If you think salt- and pepper-pots	go to 3

252

As the Olympic Express now reaches full speed again, you return to the business of trying to work out who the murderer is. You lean your head back against your comfortable seat, shutting your eyes. While you are quietly thinking like this, you hear a faint scraping sound from the direction of the door. Curious, you open your eyes again and see that a scrap of paper has been slipped into your cabin! Hoping that someone has written an important clue for you there, you eagerly pick it up. But it's not so much a clue as a boast! In an obviously-disguised handwriting, it reads: *THE MURDERER IS I. BUT YOU'LL NEVER BE ABLE TO WORK OUT WHO* I *AM!* You indignantly crumple up the scrap of paper. This has made you even more determined than ever to solve the case. ***Go to 271.***

253

Did the lead from the lamp on the table run down towards Iris or away from her?

If you think towards Iris	go to 103
If you think away from Iris	go to 272

254

You finally complete your interviews with those suspects resting in their cabins. So you can think about the answers they gave you, you decide to return to your own compartment for a while. You've just stepped through your cabin door, however, when someone grabs you from behind, clasping a wad of cotton-wool to your mouth. Immediately starting to feel drowsy, you realise that it must be steeped in some sort of lethal chemical! You're already much too weak to try and break free from the murderer but then you suddenly remember the steward's bell a little way to your left. Can your fingers reach it? You hope so – because this is your only chance of scaring the murderer off!

Record this murder attempt on your COUNTER. Now go to 282. (Remember: when there have been three murder attempts against you, this game is over and you must guess the murderer immediately.)

255

How many embroidered letters could be wholly or partly seen on the seat's headrest covers in Iris's cabin?

If you think one	go to 139
If you think two	go to 41
If you think three	go to 7

256

'Do you mind if I join you for a few minutes while you are eating?' you ask Tom Henson as you approach his table. 'Be my guest!' he replies with a wave of his hand towards the empty seat opposite him. 'This poached salmon is quite superb, by the way,' he adds. 'Why don't you have some yourself? I'll call the waiter over.' But you decline Tom's invitation, telling him that you will eat a little later perhaps . . . after all your interviews are out of the way. 'Well, what would you like to ask me?' Tom enquires genially as he pops some of the salmon into his mouth. 'Why I disliked Larry Frost so much?' As a matter of fact, that *was* what you wanted to ask him, for you simply can't understand how a man as nice as Tom could dislike *anyone*. Unless the niceness is just one big sham, of course! 'Well, I'll tell you why I disliked him so much,' Tom explains. 'He

went round saying all sorts of unfair things about me: that I couldn't act, that I was very overrated. A director like that can ruin one's career.' Now you have this answer, you decide to leave Tom to his meal. As you move towards one of the other suspects' tables, you test your memory on what you have just observed . . .

Throw the SPECIAL DICE – then turn to the appropriate number.

If	thrown	go to 143
If	thrown	go to 46
If	thrown	go to 290

257

There were four wine bottles on the ledge at the side of the mirror in the cocktail bar. Which of these was the only one containing WHITE wine?

Bottle nearest Nick	go to 212
Bottle second nearest Nick	go to 174
Bottle second furthest from Nick	go to 123
Bottle furthest from Nick	go to 284

258

When you have at last found and interviewed each of those three remaining suspects – Tom, Jacqui and Nick – you make your way back to your cabin. As you are passing from carriage to carriage, though, you have the distinct feeling that you are being followed. You turn round to check . . . but the corridor behind you is completely empty. Thinking that you must be letting your nerves get the better of you, you dismiss your suspicions. But a few seconds later there's a sudden hiss through the air. Someone has thrown a knife at your back! Will you be able to duck in time?

Record this murder attempt on your COUNTER. Now go to 47. (Remember: when there have been three murder attempts against you, this game is over and you must guess the murderer immediately.)

259

How many of the people standing around the refreshment trolley had at least one of their hands in a pocket?

If you think one go to 111
If you think two go to 31

260

As you hurry through the train, from one dark corridor to the next, you are convinced that you are gaining on the murderer. The sound of those fleeing footsteps seems to be getting nearer and nearer. You are right – because you suddenly spot the murderer at the far end of the carriage! He or she quickly turns the corner and escapes into the next carriage . . . but you are sure that you will see much more of them in this next one. Enough to identify them! As you excitedly turn the corner yourself, however, someone suddenly steps out right in front of you from one of the cabins. It's Pierre, wondering what all the commotion is about! 'You weren't to know, Pierre,' you tell him disappointedly, panting for breath, 'but I'm afraid you've let the murderer get away for the time being! The chase wasn't a complete waste of energy, though,' you add, 'I just managed to glimpse something which gives me a small clue about the person!'

You may pick up one of the coloured CLUE cards. Place it exactly over your DETECTIVE'S NOTEBOOK card to 'write down' this clue. Now go to 121.

261

What act number was chalked on the clapperboard in Larry Frost's cabin?

If you think four	go to 204
If you think five	go to 298
If you think six	go to 51

262

Making your way back to the dining-car, you peer through the glass of the partition door to see if you were right about that detail. You were! Before turning away again, you have another quick look at each of the suspects as they are eating. The thought that one of those faces belongs to a murderer quite makes you shudder! It must be a cold-blooded murderer too if he or she can now sit there consuming tea and cakes. If it had been *you* who only an hour or so ago had pushed the director off the train, you are quite sure that you would have completely lost your appetite! ***Go to 81.***

263

How far down was the blind pulled in Giles's cabin?

To top of lampshade	go to 41
To half-way down lampshade	go to 7
To bottom of lampshade	go to 232
To bottom of whole lampstand	go to 139

264

Only a few miles after leaving the station, the express enters a long tunnel. You can't wait to reach the other end. It was bad enough knowing that there was a murderer on this train before, but with the sudden pitch darkness outside and these hollow eerie noises, it seems even worse! Suddenly, the lights start to flicker in your cabin and the door creaks open. 'Pierre, is that you?' you enquire with a hopeful gulp. No, it isn't! For a large steel catapult suddenly apears round the door, held in a gloved hand. It's the murderer! You cower in the corner, hoping that he or she will miss, as you hear the thick rubber being slowly pulled back . . .

Record this murder attempt on your COUNTER. Now go to 182.

265

Which was the highest stack of newspapers on the ground?

Stack nearest newspaper-seller	go to 296
Stack furthest from newspaper-seller	go to 220

266

Tom and Iris wander further and further away from the train – Tom being the one who seems to take the lead. Is he suddenly going to break away from Iris and then make a run for it? But just as you are anxiously considering whether you should step off the train yourself and hurry after them, Tom leads Iris towards a late-night frankfurter stall on the station. After buying a glass of beer and a hot-dog for himself, he chats with Iris in front of the stall. He leans on one of the upturned wooden barrels there, happily munching away. He seems to enjoy the hot-dog much more than he did the

top-class cuisine served on the train! Perhaps he's still not quite used to being a big star yet and he yearns for the sort of life he was used to before. You watch the couple even more carefully now because Tom has at last finished his snack. What will they do now? But your fears are put at rest because they both immediately make their way back to the train. They are the first to reboard it, in fact – although the other four all arrive soon afterwards. As the train now leaves the station for the final stage of its journey, you test your memory on what you observed at the frankfurter stall.

Throw the SPECIAL DICE – then turn to the appropriate number.

If [gun] thrown go to 235

If [dagger] thrown go to 108

If [poison bottle] thrown go to 199

267

Was the boy standing on the platform holding his skis in his left or right arm?

If you think left arm	go to 79
If you think right arm	go to 252

268

Pierre now reaches the fatal door through which the director was pushed and he steps back so you can examine it. As you do so, you ask Pierre how he can feel sure that Larry Frost went overboard. You suggest to him that the shoe might have just been a red herring and the director is in fact hiding somewhere on the train, perhaps as a mean practical joke on the rest of the film team! 'No, we have proof that he fell to his doom,' the chief steward answers you firmly. 'One of the junior stewards actually *saw* him plunge into the ravine. He was polishing one of the corridor windows at the time. Quite a nasty shock it gave the poor lad, I can tell you!' ***Go to 61.***

269

In which direction was the champagne bottle pointing on Iris and Giles's table?

Towards the top of the table	go to 23
Towards the bottom of the table	go to 168
Towards Iris	go to 67
Towards Giles	go to 117

270

As you fix your eyes on the bench where Iris and Tom are sitting, you notice Iris shiver. Is this because Tom has just announced to her that he's worked out that it was *she* who pushed the director off the train? Is it because he's trying to blackmail her? But then you notice Tom shiver as well. Of course, they're both shivering because of the inadequate way they are dressed. Iris has only a thin jacket over her pullover and Tom doesn't have a jacket at all! Continuing to watch them conversing on the platform bench, you wonder why neither of them thought to pick up a coat before leaving the train. Was it because they had something else on their minds? Something much more worrying for them – like the guilt of murder, for instance! But at least the light way they're dressed

makes you confident that neither of them are intending to make a run for it. If that was the case, then they surely would have brought their coats. And, sure enough, as a whistle announces the train's imminent departure, they both step back on again. And so do all the other suspects. As the express now leaves the station, you test your memory on what you have just observed there . . .

Throw the SPECIAL DICE – then turn to the appropriate number.

If (gun) thrown go to 72

If (dagger) thrown go to 193

If (poison bottle) thrown go to 243

271

Realising that the murderer must be identified as soon as possible (if you're not to be bumped off yourself!), you decide it's time to start interviewing all the suspects. So you wander off in search of Pierre, finding him in his little office in the next carriage. 'I wonder if you could tell me the cabin number of each passenger?' you ask. Pierre is happy to oblige, immediately consulting a printed list in front of him. 'Miss Dean and Miss Carter are in the Zeus carriage, cabin numbers 3 and 4,' he tells you. 'Mr Henson and Mr Blade are in the Hercules carriage, cabin numbers 1 and 2. And – let me see now – Mr Adams and Mr Todd are in the Helene carriage, cabin numbers 6 and 7.' So it's now simply a matter of deciding which carriage to visit first . . .

If you prefer Zeus — go to 170
If you prefer Hercules — go to 246
If you prefer Helene — go to 55

272

Swaying from one carriage to the next, you manage to find three of the suspects in all. The other three cabins – those of Nick, Tom and Jacqui – are either empty or the occupants just aren't answering! Well, they can't avoid you for ever. Your paths have got to cross at some point on the train! So you're in no hurry to find these other three at the moment, making your way back to your own cabin. But as you're squeezing down the corridor, you notice some very faint writing on one of the windows, done with someone's wet finger. It concludes with the initials *L.F*. Suddenly, you work out who *L.F.* is – Larry Frost! He must have been pursued by the murderer down this corridor and, in case the worst came to the worst, he quickly left this message. It is a clue about the murderer's identity!

You may pick up one of the coloured CLUE cards. Place this exactly over your DETECTIVE'S NOTEBOOK card to find out what Larry Frost wrote about the murderer. Now go to 282.

273

Was Jacqui's right or left leg resting on the footstool in the observation car?

If you think right leg	go to 11
If you think left leg	go to 97

274

You have only just made yourself comfortable again in your cabin when there is an urgent-sounding knock at your door. When you open it, however, there is no one there. Curious, you stroll down the corridor and into the next carriage. You wonder if the person who knocked had *witnessed* the murder and meant to tell you something about it but then suddenly changed his or her mind. You can't find anyone timidly lurking in either carriage, though, and so you slowly return to your cabin. It's only when you ring the bell for Pierre a few minutes later that you make sense of this mystery, for the bell gives you a nasty electric shock. It must have been the murderer who had lured you out of your cabin so he or she could quickly tamper with the bell's wiring!

Record this murder attempt on your COUNTER. Now go to 142.

275

Which of the following city names was NOT shown on the cases's travel stickers?

If you think *BELGRADE*	go to 244
If you think *ATHENS*	go to 99
If you think *VIENNA*	go to 260

276

Before opening the door to cabin 2, you put your ear to it to listen for any movement inside. If there *is* anyone moving, then it can only be that shadowy figure, for you know this to be one of the unoccupied cabins on the train. It was used by the film team merely as a make-up room. But there isn't a sound from the other side of the door. You wonder whether you should therefore try one of the other two doors instead. But then just in case, you quickly push the door open. When you see that the cabin is empty, you are not sure

whether you are more disappointed or relieved! But then a shiver runs down your spine when you notice that one of the make-up mirrors is steamed over. Someone must have breathed over it in the last few minutes! Just as you work out that this must have been where the murderer was hiding *before* he started watching you in the corridor, someone flits past the door. The murderer again! As you start to give chase through the train, you're aware that the murderer might be trying to lure you away from the make-up cabin so he or she can creep back there and remove something. You therefore try to remember everything you saw!

Throw the SPECIAL DICE to test this memory.

If	thrown	go to 18
If	thrown	go to 124
If	thrown	go to 147

277

How many cakes were on the bottom tier of the cake stand on Iris and Jacqui's table?

If you think three	go to 3
If you think four	go to 53
If you think five	go to 192
If you think six	go to 137

278

Waiting until the express is well out of the station, you make the short walk along your corridor to the nearest washroom. While you are refreshing yourself in there, you suddenly notice that one of the paper towels has something written on it. Your eyes widen as you read. It's a desperate message from Larry Frost! It says that someone has been following him down the corridor with a gun. Although he has only obtained a brief glimpse of this mysterious person, he has a small clue as to his or her identity. He says that he is writing it down here in case the murderer finally catches up with him!

You may pick up one of the coloured CLUE cards. Place this exactly over your DETECTIVE'S NOTEBOOK card to find out what Larry Frost has written down about the murderer. Now go to 222.

279

In which direction was the umbrella handle pointing?

If you think away from Giles	go to 57
If you think towards Giles	go to 91

280

Before starting on your next series of interviews, you decide to return to your cabin for a while. You glance through the Olympic Express brochure on your seat, wondering if there's a timetable or itinerary. There is! You read that the train's next stop will be the Swiss city of Zurich. This won't be until nearly midnight, though. After that, the train does not stop until it reaches Paris at about nine o'clock in the morning, where it completes its journey. So, if you haven't worked out who the murderer is within the next twelve hours or so, it will be too late! ***Go to 162.***

281

Which object on the table was furthest from Nick?

If you think ice-bucket	go to 23
If you think ice-bucket tongs	go to 117
If you think plate of crisps	go to 168

282

You decide to delay going to find the other three suspects for a while, taking a short rest in your cabin. You feel you need it! And as a precaution, in case the murderer is hiding somewhere down your corridor, you lock your door. It isn't long, though, before you have to open it again because the express crosses the frontier into Switzerland. A customs official comes to check your passport. 'Will we be stopping at this border station long?' you ask as he stamps it for you. He tells you that the train won't be leaving for another twenty minutes and so you decide to get some fresh air. As you sit down on one of the benches right at the back of the platform, you notice that you are not the only one to have left the train. All the six suspects have done so as well! You're determined to keep your eye on them – a task made a little easier by the fact that they have split up into three pairs. Which pair should you pay *most* attention to?

If you prefer Giles and Iris	go to 294
If you prefer Tom and Nick	go to 240
If you prefer Bob and Jacqui	go to 65

283

Which letter on the express's nameplate was directly above Jacqui's beckoning finger?

If you think *X*	go to 107
If you think *P*	go to 198
If you think *R*	go to 43
If you think *E*	go to 274

284

When you have finally finished your interviews with those remaining three suspects, you decide to return to your cabin for a while. As you are making your way along the corridors, the railway line suddenly follows a sharp curve, enabling you to see one of the carriages ahead of you through the window. You notice that someone has written something in the dust on the outside of this carriage; just a single word, about a quarter of a metre high. You wonder about the significance of this word but then you realise that it is right next to the door where the murder took place. As Larry Frost was desperately hanging on to the outside of the carriage just before he fell, he must have somehow managed to write that word there as well. It's quite obvious to you now that it's a *clue* about the murderer!

You may pick up one of the coloured CLUE cards. Place this exactly over your DETECTIVE'S NOTEBOOK card to find out what this word was. Now go to 47.

285

Strolling along to the observation car, you find that Tom Henson is alone in there. He is sitting in one of the armchairs next to the large windows. You can't help feeling that his presence there is rather suspicious, however. What's the point of sitting in the observation car when it's totally dark outside? Tom seems to guess your thoughts, though. 'Must appear rather strange me sitting here when there isn't anything to see!' he remarks. 'But I came here just to get away from everyone for a while and do a bit of thinking about this murder. I thought I might be able to work out who did it!' You ask Tom if he minds *sharing* his conclusions on the subject. 'Oh, I'm afraid I had to give up with the mystery in the end,' he confesses with a chuckle. 'I was getting absolutely nowhere with it. So I decided to browse through some of the magazines here instead.'

You take your leave of Tom soon afterwards, apologising for your intrusion. 'Oh, that's all right. Anytime!' he replies genially. As you now go in search of Nick and Jacqui, you wonder if you have remembered everything about the observation car correctly. You're still a little suspicious about Tom's presence there.

Throw the SPECIAL DICE – then turn to the apppropriate number to test your memory.

If (gun) thrown go to 12

If (dagger) thrown go to 96

If (poison bottle) thrown go to 241

286

Which object on the table was furthest away from Bob?

If you think ashtray	go to 23
If you think plate of crisps	go to 117
If you think drinks menu	go to 168

287

A quarter of an hour or so after the train has left Zurich, a cream envelope appears under your cabin door. It has the Olympic Express crest on it and so you assume it has come from Pierre. You wonder if he has found out another clue about the murderer and has written it down secretly for you! So you eagerly slit open the envelope and unfold the sheet of paper inside. Too late, you realise that it has come not from Pierre but the murderer! For a strange powder falls from the paper as you open it, filling your cabin with an unpleasant smell. It must be a poison! Starting to cough and splutter, you hurriedly make your way over to the window. But you are beginning to feel drowsy already. Will you be able to pull down the window and let in the fresh air in time?

Record this murder attempt on your COUNTER. Now go to 33. (Remember: when there have been three murder attempts against you, this game is over and you must guess the murderer immediately.)

288

How far down the window was the blind pulled in Bob's cabin?

Quarter of the way	go to 91
Half-way	go to 160
Three quarters of the way	go to 254
Right to the bottom	go to 57

289

Making your way to the observation car, you find Jacqui Dean sitting in one of the plush armchairs there. She looks a lot more attractive than when you first saw her. Her distress over Larry Frost's murder was obviously very short-lived! 'My turn to be interviewed now, is it?' she asks, lifting her beautiful eyes from a magazine she is reading. 'My luck. Just when I was hoping to relax!' You begin your interview by asking Jacqui to go over precisely

what she was doing at the time Larry Frost was pushed off the train. Jacqui tells you that she was in her compartment, putting on her make-up. 'It was for the next scene we were going to shoot – the romance scene,' she explains. 'You're probably thinking that a face as beautiful as mine wouldn't need make-up,' she adds. 'Well, it doesn't really. It's just that the lights can make you look awfully pale. Anyway, I was just doing my eyes when a steward barges in to tell me that Larry appeared to have fallen from the train!' You decide that's enough questions for Jacqui for the moment, and as you go in search of Tom and Nick, you wonder how well you remember the details of what you have just observed.

Throw the SPECIAL DICE to test your memory.

If	thrown	go to 66
If	thrown	go to 219
If	thrown	go to 273

290

Was Tom drinking red or white wine with his meal?

If you think red	go to 305
If you think white	go to 13

291

'A few minutes before Mr Frost was pushed off the train,' the steward starts to inform you nervously, 'I saw him standing at the far end of the carriage corridor. I also saw someone else begin to emerge from one of the washrooms behind him. I'm sure that person was the one who pushed him off! I only had a very brief glimpse, I'm afraid, because I was suddenly called away by another of the stewards, but I did notice this about the person . . .'

You may pick up one of the coloured CLUE cards. Place this exactly over your DETECTIVE'S NOTEBOOK card to find out what the young steward has to tell you about the murderer. Now go to 81.

292

How many cakes were on the bottom tier of the cake stand on Tom and Jacqui's table?

If you think five	go to 262
If you think six	go to 178
If you think seven	go to 37

293

What was the position of Giles's legs?

Crossed at knee	go to 103
Left ankle crossed over right ankle	go to 238
Right ankle crossed over left ankle	go to 27
Legs completely uncrossed	go to 272

294

You're relieved to see that Giles and Iris haven't wandered too far from the train. In fact, they're standing right next to it, Giles with one foot still on the carriage step. He seems to be rather angry with Iris, wagging his finger at her. You wonder the reason for this. But perhaps there isn't a particular reason – for Giles Blade seems to be *permanently* cross. Just like Larry Frost was, by all accounts. It really isn't surprising that the two men didn't like each other! But did it come to rather more than just dislike, you wonder. Did it actually come to Giles pushing Larry off the train! It's at last time for the train to start moving again and you prepare to reboard it. But

you won't make a move until you're sure that all the suspects have stepped on. Tom and Nick do so as the train's whistle blows; Bob and Jacqui soon after. But Giles and Iris continue to talk on the platform. Is one of them keeping the other in conversation deliberately in the hope that the express will leave without them? Your suspicions are unfounded, though, because they both now climb into the train. As you at last do so yourself, you try to remember how Giles and Iris had been standing.

Throw the SPECIAL DICE to test whether you have all the details right.

If thrown go to 122

If thrown go to 28

If thrown go to 217

295

How many containers were on the shelf from which the three saucepans were hanging?

If you think three	go to 200
If you think four	go to 260

296

A quarter of an hour or so after leaving Zurich, you decide to go for a brief stroll along the train to allow a steward to make up the bed in your cabin. There hardly seems much point in him doing this, however. You've only eight and a half hours left to work out who the murderer is and so you're not very likely to be doing much sleeping tonight! As you wander through the train, though, it seems that most of the other passengers are now sleeping. The corridors are completely empty. Or are they? You are just entering one of the corridors when a cabin door opens at the other end. You glimpse a shadowy figure dash out of the door, then quickly disappear round the corner into the next carriage . . . ***Go to 77.***

297

Had Giles's cutlery been touched?

If you think yes	go to 3
If you think no	go to 192

298

To check whether you were right about the detail, you ring the little bell in your cabin for Pierre. 'Everything to your liking?' he asks as he appears at the door again. You tell him that you are delighted with your lavish compartment but you ask if he could show you the inside of Mr Frost's again. 'My pleasure,' he says, leading you back down the corridor and taking out his passkey. As he unlocks the door, you see that you were *right* about that detail! Pierre is just relocking the door when a junior steward comes hurrying up the corridor, asking if you're the detective. After you've nodded your head, he tells you that it was *he* who spotted the director falling from the train – and he was sure he got a glimpse of the murderer from the back. A person was hurrying away from the opened door down the corridor! You take out your notebook to record the junior steward's clue . . .

You may pick up one of the coloured CLUE cards. Place this exactly over your DETECTIVE'S NOTEBOOK card to find out what the junior steward noticed about the murderer. Now go to 21.

299

Not long after the train has left Zurich, a slip of paper is pushed under your cabin door. Curious, you pick it up and find there is a message written on the other side. It reads: *I think I know who the murderer is. Please meet me in the empty cabin 3 immediately.* You're so excited by this that it simply doesn't occur to you that it might be a trap set by the murderer. But a trap it is . . . for when you step inside the empty cabin, you're suddenly knocked over the head by a heavy instrument. The murderer was lying in wait for you behind the door!

Record this murder attempt on your COUNTER. Now go to 224. (Remember: when there have been three murder attempts against you, this game is over and you must guess who the murderer is immediately.)

300

Which part of the hand towel folded on the rail was lower?

Part in front of rail	go to 260
Part behind rail	go to 200

301

Curious, you open the note and start to read what's inside. The trouble is that it's been written in ink and a vital word has been smudged! It says: *I think I know who the murderer is. Please meet me as soon as you can in the ...... car*. The smudged word is quite a long one and so you work out that it has to be *baggage*, *dining* or *cocktail*. As you eagerly lock your cabin door behind you, delighted that this mystery could be over very soon, you wonder which of these possibilities you should decide on. Do you head for the luggage-van, the dining-car or the cocktail-car?

If you prefer luggage-van	go to 150
If you prefer dining-car	go to 85
If you prefer cocktail-car	go to 236

302

'Kindly follow me to the end of this carriage,' Pierre instructs you, starting to lead the way along the narrow corridor. 'Mind how you go,' he adds. 'These carriages are very elegant but very old as well. They rock you about much more than a modern train does.' You soon see what the chief steward means for you suddenly have to grab hold of the brass handrail as the train throws you towards the window. 'This is it,' Pierre declares uneasily when you finally arrive at the fatal door. 'This is the one through which Mr Frost was pushed!' As you bend down to examine the door, a bell suddenly rings from the next carriage. 'Would you excuse me a moment?' Pierre asks humbly. 'That bell is from one of the neighbouring

cabins. It means that a passenger wants service!' While he's gone, you test the lock on the door to make sure that it isn't broken. If it is, then maybe the director's fatal tumble *wasn't* murder at all. Perhaps it was just an accident. But the lock proves perfectly secure. Eager to ask Pierre something about the lock, you decide to go looking for him. As you stroll into the next carriage, you wonder if you have remembered all the details about the fatal door correctly . . .

Throw the SPECIAL DICE to test your memory.

If	(gun)	thrown	go to 245
If	(dagger)	thrown	go to 52
If	(poison bottle)	thrown	go to 20

303

You find yourself resting in your cabin much longer than you'd originally intended! It's a full half-hour before you feel ready to start interviewing the suspects again. You then ring the little bell in your cabin for Pierre. He arrives a few minutes later and you ask him where you can find Tom Henson, Nick Todd and Jacqui Dean. It appears that Tom is presently in the observation car and Nick in the cocktail-car. Pierre is not sure where Jacqui is at the moment but he's definite that she's not in her cabin. 'Perhaps if I sit here with my door open,' you remark thoughtfully, 'she'll come wandering past. Or I could leave her for later and go to either the observation or cocktail-car first . . .' Which will you eventually decide on?

If walk to observation car	go to 285
If walk to cocktail-car	go to 45
If wait for Jacqui	go to 186

304

How much of the word CARRIAGE was visible above the opened door?

If you think *CARR*	go to 284
If you think *CARRI*	go to 123
If you think *CARRIA*	go to 174
If you think *CARRIAG*	go to 212

305

Some forty-five minutes later you return to your cabin, having completed your interviews with those three suspects in the dining-car. On opening your door, however, you are surprised to find that the window has been pulled right down. This has made your cabin absolutely freezing! You should have been suspicious at this but you immediately walk over to the window to raise it again. It is only then that you realise that it wasn't a steward but the *murderer* who opened the window. It was to make sure you turned you back to the door! For a knife suddenly comes flying at you from that direction . . .

Record this murder attempt on your COUNTER. Now go to 47. (Remember: when there have been three murder attempts against you, this game is over and you must guess the murderer immediately.)

306

What city name was on the travel sticker on the case immediately beneath the tennis rackets?

If you think *PARIS*	go to 260
If you think *MADRID*	go to 99
If you think *BELGRADE*	go to 244
If you think *ATHENS*	go to 200